DARK
DEL

Chilling Stories with
a Wicked Twist!

This edition first published in paperback by
Michael Terence Publishing in 2025
www.mtp.agency

ISBN 9781805880608

Cover design (AI)
2025 Michael Terence Publishing

Michael Terence
Publishing

This book is dedicated to…
My lovely daughter, Rana,
my dear Granddaughter, Isabella,
& the long-suffering Hubby, John.

Contents

Jet

He rested a protective paw on Sean's knee and glared at me. Sean introduced us. 'Jet, say hello to Denise.'

The huge black Alsatian cradled his head against Sean's chest, gazing up at his master. 'You love me best,' the eyes pleaded.

Sean and I had clicked immediately, and after a few weeks we knew that it was going to be a permanent relationship. We'd started staying in more, instead of going out and spending money.

My flat was near to where we both worked. Sean's house, left to him by his parents, was several miles away in the country, so we usually ended up at my place for the evening.

We had so much in common. We both loved animals. Sean always made a fuss of my two Persian cats, and I'd been looking forward to meeting Jet, his dog.

Sean ruffled Jet's head. 'He'll come round eventually and love you as much as I do. I've had him since I was ten and he's 14 now, so he's pretty protective of me, aren't you, boy?'

Jet's tail thumped against the carpet. Then Sean leaned across to kiss me and Jet stiffened and groaned. Sean pulled away. 'It's okay, Jet. It's only Denise. She loves you too.'

But I knew that Jet would never love me.

When Sean was out, Jet stayed in the huge barn. Sean left the back doors open so that Jet could go out into a fenced-off area of garden if he wanted to.

After that first visit we called at Sean's house a couple of times. I would hear Jet whining and scratching in the barn, but Sean didn't go to see him while I was there.

Late one evening we'd been out for a drink to celebrate fixing our wedding date. We stopped at Sean's house and fell into each other's arms.

In the early hours I kissed Sean's forehead, gently brushing back a lock of hair, and I tiptoed downstairs and out the front door. Then I froze. A menacing growl echoed in the darkness. I spotted two huge amber eyes staring at me. Jet! He stood outside the barn, to the left of me. And I knew that I was in danger.

Slowly, I edged forwards, trying to reach my car and Jet started pacing towards me. As he came nearer I saw his bared teeth.

Reaching my car I managed to unlock the door despite my trembling hands, then I hurled myself inside and slammed the door shut as Jet attacked. His face stared daggers of hatred at me and oh, those eyes! Two glowing embers, burning into my brain. I'll never forget that expression as long as I live!

With a howl of disappointment, Jet turned and loped away, turning to give me a final stare.

The following day, in my flat, I broke the news to Sean. I honestly didn't wish Jet any harm. He was devoted to the man I loved, and I didn't blame him. But I obviously couldn't live under the same roof as a dog who could attack me at any time.

Sean stood up and paced the room, then he sat down and took my hand. He had a strange expression on his face that I couldn't analyse.

'Obviously I believe you, Denise,' he began, 'But are you absolutely positive that it was Jet who you saw?'

'What do you mean, am I positive? Of course I'm positive!' I snapped.

Sean breathed in deeply. 'I knew that Jet would never accept you. He'd been getting a bit crotchety lately. His arthritis was getting worse. So I took him to the vet's.' Sean's voice trembled. 'Jet died in my arms two weeks ago.'

Masterly Matches

'Hi, I'm Winston. And I'm guessing that you must be Amelia.'

'Hello Winston. Yes, c'est moi!' Amelia giggled nervously and took a glass of Champagne from a passing waiter's tray. Wow, he really had a gorgeous smile, she thought, gazing at his dark skin and his neat curly hair.

Winston helped himself to a glass. 'So tell me, what brought you here? Of course I've read your bio, but tell me yourself, in your own words.'

Amelia had a sip of her Champagne. 'I lost all my family in the pandemic, and I've been living from day to day, like a zombie. My best friend Zula filled in my details without telling me, and when I was accepted, she persuaded me to go ahead. She said it would give me something to live for. And you?'

Winston stopped smiling. 'I've no idea who my parents are, and quite frankly I don't care. They dumped me on a doorstep as soon as I was born, and I was passed from foster home to foster home.'

'Oh poor you! That's terrible!' Amelia gasped.

Winston's eyes glazed over as he relived his past. 'Not as terrible as I was! I wasn't really bad. I suppose I was just trying to attract attention to get some love and affection. The problem was, thousands of people applied to be foster parents to make some money after the first pandemic, but loads of them really weren't suitable for the job – especially when they were dealing with kids like me!'

I'd give him love, Amelia thought, bending her head down and sipping her Champagne as she felt herself beginning to blush.

'I was finally kicked out on the street when I was 14 and I joined up with a gang,' Winston continued, 'We slept in abandoned empty buildings and we ran wild. But one night my best friend Denzel was stabbed 28 times, just for the remains of a sandwich from a bin. He was covered with blood and I laid his head on my lap as he died. His last words were, Get out, Winston. Get out! And I did. I took a newspaper out of a litter bin, studied the Jobs Vacancies pages and got a job as a bouncer and night watchman in a nightclub. The owner was a real hard case, and he gave me a chance. I never went out. I ate the discarded food in the club and studied all night on the club's computers. I taught myself about self-sufficient homes, and I became fascinated with the subject. And one day I read an ad about a fallout shelter for sale under the Sussex Downs. I'd saved all my money and tips, which were often really generous, and I bought it for next to nothing. No-one else was interested in it, which surprised me. It was massive, left over from the Cold War of the 50s and 60s. I lived in it, working night and day doing up the first house and I sold it within days of advertising it, and then got the builders in to convert three more. So that's how I made my first million.' He grinned and Amelia felt butterflies quivering in her stomach as he continued speaking.

'Then came the 2nd pandemic and the Big Crash, and I lost the lot. So here I am.' He held his arms out in a helpless gesture of acceptance. Amelia wanted to rush forwards and hug him. That smile again. Oh he was gorgeous! He was over 6ft, with a broad muscular chest. His suit fitted him like a second skin.

Winston examined the lovely girl who was nearly a foot smaller than him. She had a beautiful figure and long blonde hair that reached down to her waist. He had to control his feelings. He just wanted to grab her round the waist and lead her off to bed.

'Hi there, we're Mark and Doe, but everyone calls us Make and Do!

It's often said that happy couples look like each other and it was certainly true about Make and Do.

Everyone said Hello, then Mark spoke. 'We've been self-sufficient for years.'

'We make everything ourselves out of recycled things,' Doe added.

'Doe made us a pair of matching sandals out of an old tyre once.'

'And Mark built our house, and it cost us nothing!'

Mark smiled proudly. 'Now we've made our greatest thing. Doe's pregnant!'

Amelia and Winston congratulated the couple.

'Yes and I'm 42!' she squealed happily.

'We'd tried everything but nothing worked,' Mark told them.

Doe gazed lovingly at her husband. 'I was heartbroken. I longed for a child.'

Mark grinned. 'Then we'd completely given up and we had one romantic night-'.

'Nice meal, home-made wine and a log fire-' Doe interrupted.

Mark winked at them. 'And you-know-what in front of the fire-'

His wife smiled and placed both hands on her stomach. 'So that was it. After all that tension and trying for years, one relaxed night, and it happened.'

'Do you know yet if it's a boy or a girl?' Amelia asked.

'Oh no, it's too early for that. And we want it to be a surprise!' they both exclaimed.

'I'm really looking forward to making its outfits-'

'And I'm looking forward to being a Dad now I'm old enough to be a Grandad!

'Hello, mind if we join you?'

'Not at all.' They all shuffled along a bit to make room for the new couple.

'We're Bernard and Molly,' the man told them.

Sometimes you can look at a person and guess their job at once. I bet they're farmers, Amelia thought looking at their rosy weather-beaten complexions.

'I was born a farmer, and milking my Dad's goats by the time I was three,' Bernard beamed, taking two glasses of Champagne from a passing waiter's tray and handing one to his wife. 'Molly doesn't come from a farming background, so she found it hard at first to adjust to the way of life – especially the long days. She gave the animals names. Perilous move.'

She glared at him. 'Well I couldn't help it. Baby lambs are so adorable! But I can honestly say that all our animals always had a happy life. And I did understand that they were raised to be meat. I had a couple of fields where I grew potatoes, cabbages and strawberries. And our orchard had 10 old varieties of apples and pears. And I loved my herbs, and my lovely home.' Her face grew wistful.

Winston gently questioned the couple. 'You say Had. What happened to it, if you don't mind me asking?'

Bernard shook his head. 'No, we don't mind at all. There was a loud knock on the door one night, and like a fool I opened it.'

'You must stop blaming yourself, Bernard,' Molly said and turned to the group. 'Our neighbour's cow was due to calf. We thought it was him, asking for help.'

'It was a group of marauders,' Bernard continued. 'They demanded food, money and supplies, and when I refused-' his voice broke.

Molly carried on. 'They set fire to our barns. All the animals died in agony, and the wind blew the sparks across to our house. It was hundreds of years old and it burnt like a bonfire.' Bernard put his arm round her trembling shoulders while she tried to control herself. 'The only thing I had time to rescue was our family photo, taken when our children were alive,' she whimpered.

Bernard patted Molly on the arm. 'Our neighbours were marvellous. They all rallied round to help us and our nearest neighbours put us up for as long as we wanted. Of course we worked for them. But they're all struggling to survive. And you can't impose on your friends forever, can you?'

'How awful!' Doe gasped. 'The world's gone mad!'

'You can say that again!' said a new voice. He had milk-bottle glasses, a bushy beard and his hair in a pony tail.

Computer geek, thought Amelia.

'Oh hello, I'm Carlton,' he continued, 'And this is- sorry, I've forgotten your name again, love. I've got a terrible memory for names.'

'I'm Corinna.' She glared at Carlton.

'I'm Winston, and this is-'

Carlton held up his hand. 'Waste of time. I'll forget them all at once!'

'So what do you two do?' Winston asked them.

Carlton spoke first. 'I work on computers. I love them. I can take them to bits right down to the last screw, and rebuild them with sound and a camera in them. Unfortunately it's ruined my eyesight, and my good looks.' He laughed at his own joke. Everyone politely laughed except Corinna.

Doe noticed Corinna was standing back from the group. 'And how about you, Corinna?' she asked the shy girl to include her in the conversation.

Corinna stepped forward. 'Oh I'm nothing important. I'm just a chef – or I was until recently.'

Mark spluttered, 'JUST a chef? JUST a chef? You're having a laugh aren't you? I think chefs are some of the most important people in the world!'

'As long as they don't waste anything,' Doe added, 'I can't stand waste!'

Corinna smiled cynically. 'Those days are long gone since the pandemic. There aren't many restaurants open any more, and they're all struggling. Rents are high but they have hardly any customers. Nobody makes meringues with 30 egg whites and throws the yolks away any more. And veg peelings all go in the stock pot, or to make a soup.'

'A lot of them deserved to go out of business anyway,' hollered Mark, 'I like to eat my meals with a knife and fork, not with a pair of tweezers and a magnifying glass! I wouldn't pay a fortune for a tiny square of something with a zig-zag pattern of sauce round it. Ridiculous!'

'I'm sure they can all guess that,' Doe said affectionately, patting him on the stomach. 'Onion skins are a good natural dye,' she told them all, 'And don't get me started on nettles! The Romans brought them to England and they can be used for hundreds of things, And they protect the wildlife too.'

'No, don't get her started on nettles!' Mark echoed, and everyone laughed.

Corinna stopped a passing waiter. 'Try these beef blinis,' she told everyone, taking one, 'They're delicious.'

Bernard wrinkled his nose. 'No thanks. The meat's far too young! It makes it tough. But I'll have one of these dim sum; I think that's what they're called?' The waiter nodded.

'-in fact, I'll have several. We can't be sure when we'll get our next meal.'

'How about you, Amelia?' Corinna asked.

Amelia frowned. 'With everything in short supply millions of people are suffering from malnutrition, and children are dying. I got hooked on believing that everyone is entitled to have free food. I joined several like-minded groups and we planted fruit and vegetables on waste ground. And a lot of people let us dig up their lawns, in exchange for some of the veg. Then I studied hydroponics. Fascinating. Growing things in water. I can turn a balcony into a veg garden, and a spare bedroom into an allotment.'

'That's amazing,' Winston exclaimed, 'I built all my houses with extra space for growing their own food underground, but I never knew what to put in there, so I left it up to the buyers.'

'Excuse me,' Carlton interrupted, 'I'm going to talk to the surgeon and his family. They're all doctors. His two daughters got married a few days ago. Normally they would have had hundreds of guests, but not nowadays, of course. It's not allowed any more. One of their husbands is a doctor, and the other one's a dentist. Talk about keeping it in the family! Come on, er-'

'Corinna,' she snapped.

He walked off with Corinna tailing behind him, clutching her Champagne and her blini.

'Beautiful costumes,' Doe remarked, 'So colourful!' Everyone agreed with her.

Amelia sighed. 'Shame about the weddings though.'

There was a sudden beeping noise and a voice bellowed out of the loudspeakers. 'Hello everyone! Thank you all for coming here today. Will you now take your places as we're about to commence.'

With comments of See you later, the group split up and they wandered away in different directions.

The catering staff bustled around, collecting the food and glasses.

Bernard and Mark each grabbed a handful of canapes and ate them as they walked.

Amelia tugged on Winston's wrist. 'Where's Carlton? she asked, staring round the room.

Winston pointed across the room. 'Over there, still in deep conversation with the surgeon and his family. Why?'

Amelia spoke quietly. 'I don't think Corinna likes him very much.'

Lightly shrugging one shoulder, Winston said, 'Opposites attract. And they're both interesting people. I'm sure they'll click when they get to spend more time alone, talking to each other. Anyway, he might be dynamite in bed!' He stared straight at Amelia, watching her colour change. Amelia looked down at the floor to hide her red cheeks. She was cross with herself, blushing like a schoolgirl. She looked up and gazed straight into Winston's brown eyes. He had an amused half-grin on his face and she couldn't stare him out. She scrutinized the room until she felt her face grow cooler.

Winston took hold of Amelia's hand. 'How about sitting over there?' he asked, nodding at a red double sofa. Amelia agreed and they walked towards the seat.

'This is comfy,' Amelia declared, bouncing up and down. 'It's nice and squishy.'

I'm behaving like a schoolgirl again, she thought. But I don't care any more.

'Yes, it is.' Winston bounced up and down beside her. 'Why is it often so difficult to find a comfortable seat? I'm sure the designers have different-shaped bums to me.'

Amelia sighed happily, feeling a warm rush of contentment, 'I think that a lot of seats are designed to discourage people to sit on them for long, but they've certainly succeeded with this one. I could sit here for ages.' Then her words tailed off.

Winston put his arm round her shoulders. 'Amelia, I fancy you like mad,' he whispered. His face came nearer and nearer and he kissed her tenderly on the lips. She linked her arm round his neck and eagerly returned the kiss. Yes, they were definitely a Masterly Match, she conceded.

Then the earth moved; literally, as the five immense engines fired up, struggling to raise the massive heavy rocket off the ground and into the air. It elegantly rose upwards, rapidly gaining maximum speed with a long tail of fire behind it, then safely blasted through the Van Allen belts, leaving the dangerous, devastated world behind for ever.

It was beginning its nine months' journey, transporting the group of pioneering passengers away through Outer Space to colonise the planet Mars.

Mother Knows Best

Completely disinterested, she gazed round her expensive modern kitchen.

Garth liked everything to be perfect. He always tried to create a good impression.

He would come home with all the latest gadgets, then he got impatient with her when she didn't use any of them and they never came out of the cupboards.

He was always getting impatient with her.

'Why do you keep using all that tatty old rubbish?' he'd say, 'Everything takes you so much longer.'

She couldn't make him understand that her Mother's kitchen equipment was well worn through constant loving use. Most of it had belonged to her Grandmother when she was alive. She hadn't even had electricity in her cottage, let alone time-saving gadgets!

Mother always said that there was a lot more to baking than just whizzing things up in a machine. It needed gentle coaxing and love to produce perfect results.

Lifting her Mother's old mixing bowl out of the cupboard, she placed it on the table.

It was heavy, and worth a lot of money now. Oh what a lot of memories it revived, of kneeling on a stool while Mother expertly mixed everything. Then she'd scrape it into a baking tin and lift up the bowl as though carrying it to the sink and after pretending to ignore her daughter's protests, she would replace the bowl on the table with a smile, giving her the spoon to lick.

Carefully weighing out the ingredients for her Mother's old gingerbread recipe, she tipped them in the bowl one by one, pausing to check her recipe all the time in case she forgot something.

She measured out the dry ingredients first; half brown and half white sugar, plain flour carefully sieved to remove any lumps, ground ginger, a pinch of nutmeg, a larger pinch of cinnamon, bicarb of soda, and a tiny pinch of salt.

The bouquet from the spices was irresistible. She bent over the bowl and inhaled. Lovely, and all natural. Mother Nature was so clever!

And then the wet ingredients; I beaten egg, and 6 tablespoons of treacle trickled in to make the mixture easy to handle.

Taking her Mother's old wooden spoon out of the drawer under the table, she stirred everything together slowly, carefully and thoroughly. She never used an electric mixer. Mother always said that any food preparation had to come from the heart, along the arms, and through the fingers.

And then finally she added her Mother's secret ingredient.

I'm sorry, but I'd have to kill you if I told you what it is!

Garth loved her gingerbread. He didn't love her Mother, but he loved her old recipes. And it was his birthday, so she thought she'd make it a memorable day for him.

Of course, he wouldn't come straight home from the gym. He'd say that some of the other self-obsessed, fake tanned, hairless, waxed, unnaturally bloated freaks had insisted on treating him to a few drinks for his birthday. She'd never met any of them and she didn't want to. What would they talk about? She had nothing in common with them at all. And Garth had never invited her to meet them. It was his world, kept completely separate from their home life.

But she'd seen them all trickling out of the building singly or in pairs when she'd sat on a park bench in the grounds, opposite the entrance, watching for him to come out. None of them had noticed her though. He was often much later than the others.

It was an expensive country club, with gym, pool, restaurant, function rooms for weddings and events, and bedrooms upstairs. She'd never been inside it.

He never came straight home after a workout. But he always had a shower to remove all the stink, and splashed on his deodorant, cologne, etc so he smelled nice and fresh. A lot of them were free samples and he enjoyed trying them out. Some of them smelt awful.

She could smell him right through the front door before he came in, it was so strong.

Using her hands, which she'd rinsed under the tap to make sure they were cold and clean, she formed everything into a ball, making sure that she scraped up all the dough round the bowl. She floured the board, which was discoloured and slightly warped from years of constant use by her Mother, slapped down the raw mixture, giving it an extra pat to make it smooth and rolled it out with her Mother's old wooden rolling-pin.

Picking up her Mother's old scalpel, she cut out the gingerbread man's shape as exact as she could.

She outlined the expensively styled shoulder-length curly hair, then the bulging biceps, built up by long gym sessions and steroids. And she cut out a small willy, poking it into shape, and laughing. Steroids and workouts might improve a six-pack, but they didn't make any difference to some parts of the anatomy, she thought, moulding two tiny feet. Apparently the size of a man's feet reveals a lot about other organs.

Gently squeezing the spare dough together, she cut out a gingerbread woman. Her face was in profile, staring lovingly at the gingerbread man and, like Garth, she had an unnaturally shaped body with bulging muscles. It also had a skinny waist and big surgically-enhanced boobs.

Placing both shapes side by side on a tray, she baked them in the hot oven for 10 minutes, so they were cooked but still soft, but with no soggy bottoms, ha ha!

Gingerly lifting the gingerbread man onto a plate with a spatula, she rested her hands on the table and leaning forward she stared at it, concentrating her thoughts until she lost track of time. Yes, he looked perfect!

She picked up her Mother's old tin of pins. They were longer than the usual dressmaking pins, with tiny coloured balls on the end. She removed the lid and stuck two pins in the biscuit's tiny feet, two in its thighs, and one in the willy, making sure it went right through and giving it an extra twist. Then she carried on upwards with two in the kidneys, two in the bulging biceps, one in the heart, one in the throat, straight through the Adam's Apple and two in the eyeballs.

Grinning, she began to sing, 'Happy Birthday to You. Happy Birthday to You. Happy Birthday dear Garth, Happy Birthday to You' while she lifted up the biscuit and removed the pins one by one. Daintily holding it on the palm of her hand, she inhaled the fresh gingery odour, then she bit off one of the legs and chewed it slowly.

'Mm, yummy,' she muttered, raising her head and closing her eyes for a moment, 'Mother would definitely approve!'

***

'When are you going to leave her, Garth?'

'I keep telling you soon, Luv, soon.'

'That's what you keep saying. You keep promising me but you never do anything about it!'

'I'm working on it. It's not easy.'

'Why not? It's easy enough. What's the problem? Just pack a case and go!'

'Not now, eh? Please stop talking. I'm trying to concentrate.'

'Oh Garth, I love your body sooooo much! And you love my body too, don't you? We go so well together. You do love me the best, don't you, Garth? You don't love her, do you? You said you didn't.'

'Aaagh!'

'What's wrong darling?'

'I've got cramp in my thigh. And pins and needles in my feet. Aagh, it's really bad!'

'Oh, don't get off me now! I'm nearly there! Oh, hang on, please! Keep moving, Garth darling!'

'Aagh, now it's in the other one!'

'Well work through the pain. Just keep going. Don't stop! We haven't got much time. You'll be leaving soon, won't you, spending your birthday with Her!'

'I can't keep going if you keep yapping. It's - AAAGH!'

'Garth! Garth! What's wrong? Are you alright? Garth! Oh my God, why is he making that gurgling noise? Garth, get off me! You're squashing me! I can't move, you're so heavy! You're a dead weight. Garth? Garth!'

***

She didn't stick pins in the gingerbread woman. She picked it up and bit off the head, holding it in her mouth until it began to dissolve. Then she chewed and chewed until there was nothing left.

Mother had often said that you should always chew your food at least 20 times.

***

'Garth, I'm choking! My throat's closing up! Help, I feel as though my head's bursting open! Garth! You're suffocating me. You're so heavy! My body's going all numb. Aaagh, Garth! Somebody help me!'

The last thing she heard was footsteps thumping up the uncarpeted oak stairs and fists hammering at the door.

***

Swallowing the gingerbread foot, she daintily used a pin as a toothpick. Then she wiped it clean, dropped it in the tin and replaced the lid.

She was washing up the baking things when the phone rang and she smiled, drying her hands on a towel.

Before she answered it, she knew what the news would be. She'd been expecting a call.

Mother always said that she should never have married him and she'd be better off without him.

She'd hated him on sight. She'd refused to come to the wedding, which was upsetting. So in the end they'd had a quiet wedding with no family or friends.

Yes, Mother was always right. She should have listened to her instead of being fooled by his good looks and his smarmy charm.

How had she put up with him for so long? After all, Mother knew best!

Mr Oak

'Can I sleep in your bed, Barney? I'm scared. Tel's hitting Mum again.'

Barney pulled his duvet back so Crystal could climb in beside him. He put his arms round his sister, then they both trembled as a loud voice bellowed up the stairs.

'Come down here you useless kids!' Tel roared.

'No Tel, leave them alone!' whined their mum.

'Down. Now!' Tel repeated up the stairs, then he tripped over. He burped and pulled himself onto his feet, leaning on the banister.

'I don't want to go down there,' Crystal whispered with tears in her eyes.

Barney helped her out of the bed. 'We've got no choice, Crystal,' he said, 'If we don't, he'll come up here and start hitting us and that'll be worse.'

Tel was swaying around with a can of lager in his hand. There was blood down the front of his football shirt.

Their mum was cowering and whimpering on the ground, her right eye turning black.

'Did your team lose again?' Barney bravely asked, stepping in front of Crystal.

'You cheeky little brat!' snarled Tel, lunging at the boy with his fists clenched. Crystal screamed.

'Quick kids, run!' shrieked their mum, grabbing hold of Tel's shirt and hanging on while he tried to shake her off.

Barney took hold of Crystal's hand and, opening the back door, ran along the garden path.

A tall oak tree stood at the bottom of the garden. It was over 300 years old. It had a preservation order on it and it had to be left alone and untouched when the row of terraced houses was built.

The old tree was hollow and Barney and Crystal often used it as a hiding place when Tel was drunk.

Barney kept a collection of things for survival inside the old tree; a blanket, a couple of cushions and a bottle of water which he refilled regularly.

'Get back here you pathetic brats - now!' Tel was yelling out the back door.

'No Tel, leave them alone! Come on, come to bed,' their mum coaxed him.

The back door slammed and Barney and Crystal settled down inside the tree for the night.

It was cosy and comfortable in their hiding place and they felt safe and protected as they fell asleep.

The sun's rays gently awoke them in the morning and they crawled out of the tree, feeling refreshed and content.

Tel would be snoring in bed until midday so they were safe for the morning.

They heard a voice and they peeped over the fence. Laetitia, their neighbour, was singing to her plants, turning in circles with her arms stretched out. Her multicoloured clothes swirled and floated around her.

'Hello my lovely children of the tree!' she called, approaching the fence and blowing them kisses from her hand, 'That dreadful man was drunk again last night, wasn't he?'

Barney nodded. 'Yes, his stupid team lost again. Ooh, I HATE him so much!'

Laetitia reached her arms up towards the sky. 'Well I've put a strong curse on him. I don't usually do bad spells, only good ones. But in this case I've made an exception.'

'Thank you,' said Barney, not knowing what else to say. He started to walk away, then he paused.

'Um. Laetitia,'

'Yes, my darling,' Laetitia replied.

'Do trees have feelings? I mean, do they know when we're talking to them?'

'Of course they do!' Laetitia smiled,' They're aware of everything that's going on around them. This is being accepted now by people who used to scoff at ideas like that. They've discovered that trees link their roots together and pass on knowledge of their surroundings to each other, for miles, all across the land. And when we mess with Nature we're doing a lot of harm to them. Trees are very important on this planet.'

'So Mr Oak knows if I talk to him.'

Laetitia held her arms out over the fence. The two children rushed over and were enclosed in her embrace. Barney closed his eyes and inhaled. Laetitia emitted a glorious perfume of herbs, baked bread, freshly mown grass and summer evenings. Her voice was so soothing. 'Of course he does, my dears. He hears every word you say. Doesn't he look after you both and protect you when you hide inside him?'

Barney nodded. 'Yes, I think he does.'

'I love Mr Oak,' said Crystal.

'Well there you are then! He's your best friend and he loves you very much. And so do I! I'll cast another spell this evening to help to protect you both. It's Halloween, so my spells will have extra power.'

Laetitia waved goodbye and started to sing again.

Their mum was setting out breakfast bowls. 'Ssh, don't wake him,' she warned.

Tel shuffled in while they were eating their cereal. He was scratching his fat belly under a filthy white vest and underpants with footballs on. 'Is there anything to drink around here?' he asked, hunting in the fridge.

He glared at the two children. 'Oh you're back,' he snarled, I'm sick of you kids hiding from me. I'm going to put a stop to it once and for all!'

He went into the shed and then waddled down the garden, carrying a chainsaw.

'No! yelled Crystal, running after him, 'You can't hurt Mr Oak!! and she kicked him on the shin.

'Oh can't I? Just you watch me!' Tel shouted, hopping on one leg and pushing Crystal onto the ground. Barney helped her up, glaring at Tel.

Laetitia looked over her fence and spotted him. She stuck out her right arm and pointed at him. She called, 'You can't touch the tree. It's protected!'

'Shut up you old witch!' Tel retaliated. He started the chainsaw and approached the oak.

Barney and Crystal screamed as he held the saw against the tree. The teeth easily bit into the ancient dried bark.

Suddenly, a branch curled round his arm. He didn't notice it at first. It pushed the chainsaw towards him.

Tel gradually realised that he was trapped, but he couldn't control his arm and he couldn't get free. He struggled but the chainsaw drew nearer and nearer. He finally shrieked as he cut his own head off. It ended with a short gurgle.

Laetitia smiled and hummed a little tune, waving her hands in front of her.

Barney and Crystal's mum grabbed hold of Crystal and buried the girl's face against her chest, while letting out a moaning noise.

The head dropped on the ground and rolled towards Barney. He watched it, fascinated, as it drew nearer. It stopped right in front of him. It had a frozen grin on its face. He looked down, then he drew his foot back, and kicked the head up in the air and over the fence at the end of the garden.

'Gooooooalll!' he shouted.

Nancy the Nymphomaniac Ghost

'Darling, how could you BEAR to live in this ghastly place?'

Martin Bramley closed his eyes and shuddered. Her voice had an effect on him like fingernails scraping down a brick wall.

'Because I happen to LOVE it, Stephanie DARLING!' he snapped. But his sarcasm was wasted on her, as usual.

'But it's so spooky, darling. And what was that dreadful group of people called who used to have drunken orgies here?'

'The Hellfire Club.' Martin grinned. 'Actually I'm thinking of reviving their practices. They really knew how to have fun, Steph DARLING!'

'Really Martin,' she sighed, looking at her watch. 'You can be so childish sometimes. And don't call me Steph. It's so common.'

Suddenly he wanted to grab her by the throat and shake her. But it would only cause problems. Instead he said, 'Funny isn't it how everything I say in my cockney accent is to common, but you fall about shrieking with laughter when your ponsy pals say Oh Fuck! In their stuck-up voices!'

But it was water off a duck's back. She just tutted and sighed, then she said, 'I'm not getting into one of your silly arguments, Martin. I've got to go. Gerald is taking me out to dinner.'

'Oh good old Gerald!' he shouted, then he walked over to the kitchen worktop and pouring himself a double whisky, he took a large swig. He instinctively tensed, and waited for her usual disapproving comments, but she didn't say anything.

Stephanie clomped loudly across the oak floor in her stiletto heels, making Martin wince at the noise and the possible damage to the old floorboards. She opened the front door and then she paused. 'Are you <u>sure</u> you'll be alright, darling?' she asked him.

Martin smiled. 'Yes, thank you. I'll be fine.' Once you've gone, darling.

'Well as long as you're sure.' She looked down at the floorboards. 'And do get a carpet fitted, Martin. These floors are so noisy, and draughty too, I expect.' Then she slammed the door (Stephanie always slammed doors) and he heard her footsteps echoing away along the corridor and down the oak stairs.

Letting out a large sigh of relief, Martin took a large gulp of whisky, then he topped up his glass.

Raising his glass he said aloud, 'Cheers Gerald. And thanks a lot, pal!'

What the hell had he seen in her? And, even stranger, what had she, the fashion editor of a women's magazine, seen in him, a humble bus driver?

Even on the honeymoon he knew that he'd made a mistake. But Stephanie didn't seem to think so. She didn't need to. She always got her own way. Always. They never rowed, she'd just make a comment like, 'Don't be silly darling,' making him feel stupid and inferior, much to his own disgust.

Martin had often tried to tell her that he was leaving her, but even though he detested her, he couldn't pluck up the courage. It seemed that he was stuck with darling Stephanie for life.

Imagine his surprise and joy then when Stephanie came home from work and told him, 'Darling, I've got something to tell you. I want a divorce. I <u>do</u> hope you won't be too upset!'

'I'll try not to be,' he'd replied, fighting back his smirk.

The three of them had decided to sit down together and discuss things in a civilised manner. Martin was delighted with the results. Gerald had paid him for his half of the house and furniture, plus a very generous moving allowance, enabling him to buy a top-floor apartment in the newly-converted Amberley Abbey.

Martin thought the large Gothic building was beautiful; a very fair swap for darling Stephanie and that semi-detached beige glass box!

His apartment was obviously originally the servants' quarters, now with several rooms knocked into one.

There was a large open-plan kitchen and living area, and a small bedroom that was barely big enough for the huge old oak bed that he'd bought at an auction. The ceiling sloped, so he would have to be careful not to bang his head when he got out of bed.

Pouring himself another whisky, he mimicked Stephanie's voice; 'Oh darling, do you really think you should? Don't you think you've had enough?'

She'd disapproved of his having a couple of drinks at home in the evening, but it was alright for her to pour a non-stop stream of Martinis down her throat at one of her dreadful friends' dreadful parties!

Hypocritical bitch. 'Here's to freedom, and up yours, Steph, DARLING!' he declared, downing the whisky and pouring another one.

He was beginning to feel a bit woozy and the room was swaying slightly. He stood up, finished his whisky, turned off the electric log-effect fire and walked unsteadily into the bedroom.

Undressing, he climbed naked into the bed, being careful not to bang his head on the ceiling. He'd never been allowed to sleep naked with Stephanie. He couldn't remember why.

Lying on his back, he stared at the lights from the communal gardens reflecting through the window onto the sloping ceiling. Relaxed and content, he started to drift into unconsciousness.

Then he felt the duvet move and a draught of cold air.

Fully awake, he tensed and listened. Then he relaxed again and closed his eyes. Too much whisky, old son, that's what's wrong with you, he thought.

And he felt lips, travelling lightly over his chest.

Lips? Ridiculous! Must be a spider or a mosquito or something. The old building was probably full of them.

But he knew that it wasn't a spider or a mosquito; it was a Something. And the sensation was too enjoyable to disturb as the lips kissed and nibbled their way downwards until-

'Aah!' he sighed. This was ecstasy! He didn't understand what was happening, but he was too happy, and too drunk to care.

The phantom lips stopped. And something lowered itself on top on him. Instinctively he tried to put his arms round the body, but there was no body there, and there was nobody there either! No living body, anyway. Just a change in the temperature, which had dropped, and weight of the air; a chemical suggestion of a body.

Martin stretched his arms out beside him and tried to relax. 'I'm having sex with a ghost,' he sighed, 'I'm screwing a spook. And it's WONDERFUL!'

He came with a silent shudder, and he felt the bedclothes move again.

The sexy ghost had gone.

***

Had it been an alcohol-induced experience? It must have been a dream, surely! But Martin knew deep down that it hadn't been a dream. It had really happened.

His friends invited him for a drink after work, but he'd refused. 'I've still got a load of work to do in the flat,' he told them.

He bought some fish and chips and washed them down with a couple of cans of lager. Then he looked at his watch. It wasn't 9 o'clock yet. So what? He could do what he bloody well wanted to do now that he was free. If he decided to go to bed at 9 o'clock it was his business!

Although he wasn't the slightest bit tired, Martin stripped off and stretched out on his back in the bed.

After a few minutes, he felt ridiculous lying there, waiting for a ghost to get into bed with him, and he snorted with embarrassed laughter.

Then the room went cold, and the duvet lifted. And the lips started nibbling at his skin. Over his face, round his neck and across his chest they played, teasing their way gently downwards.

With a contented sigh, he closed his eyes and let his body be taken over, enjoying every part of the experience.

They weren't like living lips; it was more like having a butterfly travelling over him, flying up and landing again on another part of his body. It kissed and nipped him with a light pressure. But oh, the pleasure was more than light!

He lifted the duvet and looked down. But there was nothing to see, only his own erection propping up the bedclothes.

Martin wondered who the ghost was. Had she been an eager participant in the Hellfire Club orgies? Or did she date back a lot further, to when Amberley Abbey had been a convent?

Was she a red-hot hooker, or a frustrated nun? He christened her Nancy; Nancy the Nymphomaniac Ghost.

He'd always liked older women. They were free of hang-ups and more experienced than young girls.

But was he having sex with someone who was around 700 years old now? That's what you call an older woman!

Well, he'd never know, and whoever she was, she sure knew what she was doing! So he may as well relax and let Nature take its course. Good old Nature!

'Wow, get in there, Nancy,' he sighed, 'Go on, go on, down a bit, that's it, right there!'

When he gently and effortlessly shuddered to a climax, he laughed out loud. Who cares? he thought, the walls are thick. Talk about getting into the spirit! He hoped she wouldn't have a phantom pregnancy!

He chuckled to himself as he fell asleep. Sex without sweat. Even darling Stephanie would enjoy that!

***

What was the time? He raised his arm and looked at his watch. 3am. What had jerked him awake? He felt a cold draught and the duvet lifted. Oh no, not again – well, not so soon!

He tried to pull the duvet down. 'Not now, Nancy,' he said, 'I've got to be up in three hours' time for work.'

The duvet was pulled aside and the ghostly lips began their journey downwards.

Martin wriggled, trying to shake off the phantom form. But no luck. He was pinioned onto the mattress on his back while his sexy room-mate had her way with him.

He had no choice but to accept it until he came, but he wasn't so excited this time.

'Now float off and leave me alone,' he pleaded, rolling onto his side. The duvet lifted and Nancy departed again.

Martin lay awake for a while, thinking. It wasn't so enjoyable now, especially if he could be used whenever the ghost wanted him! What was he going to do?

***

'No, not tonight, Nancy, please!' Martin protested as the spirit lips started their journey down his chest. 'It's very nice, don't get me wrong, but it's been at least once a night for over two weeks now. I'm going to sleep. I'm knackered.' He tried to turn on his side, and he found that he couldn't. He was forced on his back again and he was unable to resist the invisible pressure.

'Christ,' he muttered as the ghostly vagina descended on top of him, 'I'm being raped by my own imagination!'

He tried to push the ghost off him, although he knew that he was wasting his time. His hands went straight through the air.

With a sigh, he gave up the ghost and lay back. 'Okay Nancy,' he told his phantom partner, 'You get on with it and help yourself. I'm going to sleep. In fact, I'm so exhausted that I can't stay awake, whatever you do.'

***

'What's up with you lately, Martin? The divorce upset you, did it?'

'Eh? Oh no, Keith. It's not that. I'm enjoying my freedom.'

'Well it's only been six weeks, hasn't it? I was dead chuffed when I got my divorce, but it still had an effect on me afterwards. You know, I wasn't used to being on my own and fending for myself. Come on, let's go for a pint. You look as though you need one.'

Keith went to get the beers and Martin pointed to a table in the far corner of the pub. 'Let's go and sit over there, Keith, where it's quieter,' he said, I want to tell you something. I've got to talk to someone!'

While Martin blurted out everything about the ghost, Keith sat silently frozen with his mouth hanging open and his glass half-raised to his mouth.

'You-you're joking!' Keith spluttered when Martin had finished. 'You are joking, aren't you? I mean, you can't be serious! A nymphomaniac ghost Martin! It's impossible!'

Martin just sat silently, miserably looking at his friend.

'You do look well and truly knackered though, I must admit,' Keith continued, 'And you've lost weight. You don't seem to be kidding. It's just so hard to believe.' He put his glass down and stroked his chin for a moment. 'I tell you what!' he said at last.

'What?' Martin asked, stifling a yawn.

'You could obviously do with a good night's sleep. Why don't you spend the night in my flat-' He licked his lips '-and I'll stay in yours.'

Martin's face lit up. 'Oh Keith, would you?'

Keith smiled with eager anticipation. 'Sure. Anything for a Mate.'

***

Gawd, what a spooky place, Keith thought as he shut the door behind him and switched the light on. Mysterious shadows were cast on the high carved ceiling and in corners of the room, and Keith felt nervous.

Martin had told him to help himself to anything he wanted, and he gratefully poured himself a large whisky, topping it up with water. After a couple of warming mouthfuls slipped down into his stomach, he felt a bit better.

'I must be mad,' he told himself, speaking out loud to give himself courage, 'A nympho ghost? Martin's playing a practical joke on me. But still, he did look bad!'

The silence and the shadows made him feel uneasy, so he turned the fire on, and then switched on the TV and watched a film while he ate his takeaway curry.

After a final glass of whisky, he turned the bedroom light on and switched everything off in the lounge.

'Look out darlin' here I come,' he muttered, completely undressing, turning off the light and climbing into bed.

He lay spread out like a serious sunbather and waited. Then the irony of the situation hit him. He could imagine

Martin picturing him in bed, waiting for a non-existent nymphomaniac ghost to get under the duvet with him, and he burst out laughing. I've been well and truly had, he thought, but not like I expected to be had!

Then the duvet lifted and a cold draught blew into the bed.

Keith stiffened – everywhere! He trembled with fear and anticipation as the phantom lips tickled their way across his chest, and down, down, until – 'Aaagh!' Keith yelled as a set of ghostly gnashers clamped onto the end of his organ and stayed there.

He leaped out of bed and ran into the lounge, performing frenzied movements like a demented disco dancer and spinning round in circles. But still the phantom teeth hung on tight.

Gradually he moved towards the front door, and he opened the door, hoping the pain would subside when he was out of the ghost's territory. He poked his painful willy into the landing and sighed with relief as the pressure stopped. He turned back into the room, and then suddenly, before he realised what was happening, he was jerked onto his knees on the landing and the door slammed shut.

'Oh no!' he cried, pushing against the door, but it was hopeless. He was locked out, naked and helpless. And he might need hospital treatment for his injuries. But how on earth was he going to explain what had caused them? 'I was bitten by a nympho ghost and I'm worried that it might be infected.'

***

Martin was given a lot of suspicious looks by his passengers while driving his bus the next day, because every time he thought about Keith and his night at Amberley Abbey, he burst out laughing.

Keith was given a lot of suspicious looks too because he kept staring down at the front of his trousers while he drove along. He was checking to see if he'd swollen up.

Martin had been in a deep, refreshing sleep when a wild-eyed Keith burst into his own flat at around 5am. He was clutching himself with both hands. 'She bit me!' he kept saying.

'What? Who? Where?' Martin asked, trying to drag himself into consciousness.

'Her. Here.' Keith pointed to the front of his trousers. 'Your jealous ghostly girlfriend. Bit me, she did!'

'Oh dear.' Martin struggled to hide his laughter, and he started to get up. 'Do you want your bed back?' he asked.

Keith shook his head. 'No, you stay there. I'm going to soak myself in a bath with disinfectant. Can you catch gangrene or tetanus from a ghost?'

'No idea,' Martin snorted, 'I don't know anyone who has been bitten by one. So tell me what happened.'

'She bit me and wouldn't let go. And then she pushed me out onto the landing and slammed the door,' Keith called from the bathroom while he ran a bath.

'Well how did you get back in?' Martin asked him when he reappeared.

'I huddled on the floor all night as the heating had gone off. I was freezing! Then a young couple came out of the apartment opposite yours at 5ish with some suitcases. They were off to Gatwick to catch a plane. And they looked at me and said, Morning as though it was the most natural thing in the world to see a naked man outside your door. Very polite and British! I had to stop them and ask them to send someone up with a key to let me in. Then I grabbed all my stuff and got out of there quick. Here's your key. And before you ask, yes I believe in ghosts now, and I hope I never encounter another one again as long as I live!'

After he'd stopped laughing, Martin finally managed to nod off to sleep again for another hour, while Keith had his bath and sat in an armchair with the light on, regularly checking himself for any change in size or colouring. The teeth marks gradually faded to a dark rosy pink, but he still anxiously kept staring at it.

When he woke up, Martin made a decision. He couldn't share a flat with a jealous nymphomaniac ghost for the rest of his life. She was wearing him out. He had to sell it.

So he went to see Swizzle and Bull the Estate Agents in his lunch break and gave them details of the apartment (except about Nancy) and left them a spare set of keys.

He wondered how quickly it would sell. Mr Swizzle said that there was a waiting list for property in that area.

***

'Well here we are, Amberley Abbey. Marvellous tastefully converted building, as I'm sure you'll agree.'

'Oo yes, Mr Swizzle, it looks super, doesn't it, Cyril?'

'Super, Denise.'

'Cyril and I are getting married in June and we want to prepare our own home first, don't we, Cyril?'

'We do, Denise.'

'And I'm sure that Amberley Abbey will be just the right home for you. Shall we go inside?'

'Oo yes, come on, Cyril.'

'I'm coming, Denise.'

Mr Swizzle paused outside the main double doors. 'Just one thing before we go in. Mr Bramley, the owner, has stipulated emphatically that he would like all viewing to be done in silence. He wants no discussions of any kind to take place on the premises.'

'Oo, that's a bit strange, Mr Swizzle, isn't it, Cyril?'

'Very strange, Denise.'

'No, no, it's not strange at all, let me assure you! There is a logical explanation. Mr Bramley said that his neighbours are so nice that he doesn't want them to have any inkling yet that he's moving. So if you don't mind, we'll go inside casually, as though we're friends of his, view the property in silence, and then we'll return to my office to answer any of your questions and discuss the details.'

'Oo, now we understand, don't we, Cyril?'

'Yes, perfectly, Denise.'

They explored Martin's apartment with silent admiration, pointing out things of interest, and mouthing Oos and Aahs to each other. Then, when they'd explored everywhere, Denise, said, 'It's gorgeous. We'd like to buy it, wouldn't we, Cyril?'

'Yes we would, Denise.'

'Fine, we'll go back to my office and get the legalities sorted out. And I'm sure we don't need to worry about the neighbours hearing us now,' Mr Swizzle stated, rubbing his hands together.

***

'Mr Bramley?'

'Speaking.' Mr Swizzle had left a message on Martin's phone and he returned the call in his first break. Was it a sale already? He felt optimistic. After all, it was a beautiful apartment in a lovely historical building, and he'd asked for a slightly higher price than he'd paid for it.

'Albert Swizzle here of Swizzle and Bull, Estate Agents, Limited. Thank you for returning my call.'

'Hello Mr Swizzle. Sold my flat already, have you?'

'No Mr Bramley, I have <u>not</u> sold your apartment! In all my years as a professional Estate Agent, I have suffered a number of setbacks, which is only to be expected from time to time with this job. I've waded through mud and sewage, I've been chased by savage dogs, my head has narrowly missed being cut open by falling tiles, and I've suffered the indignity of getting stuck halfway through a floor with dry rot. But I've never, never experienced a situation like the one that my clients and I experienced today.'

Martin swallowed nervously. 'Situation?' he asked.

'Situation, Mr Bramley. You omitted to inform me that your apartment was inhabited by ghosts.'

'Ghosts?'

'Ghosts, Mr Bramley. As soon as the poor lady told me that she and her fiancé wanted to buy your property, she was attacked by half a dozen eggs in rapid succession, followed by an egg whisk.'

'An egg whisk?' Sounds like Nancy was inviting them to make an omelette, Martin thought.

'An egg whisk, Mr Bramley. It chased her out of the lounge and through the front door. The poor lady ran screaming along the corridor, narrowly avoiding being struck on the back of the head by a large book entitled Cookery For One. And as for the poor man…'

This could be nasty. 'What happened to the poor man?'

There were faint noises at the other end of the phone as though Mr Swizzle was being strangled before his voice was heard again. 'It snatched his toupee off.'

'His toupee?' Martin tried desperately not to laugh.

'His toupee, Mr Bramley. Snatched right off his head it was. And it ran along the floor like a little Pekinese while the poor man tried to catch it. And when he bent down to pick it up, he was tripped up by a footstool.'

'A footstool?'

'A footstool, Mr Bramley. Meanwhile the lady, who was distressed enough as it was, peeped round the door and started to scream that her fiancé had been scalped! It seems that she didn't know about the toupee. And as for myself-'

Oh dear. 'What happened to you, Mr Swizzle?'

Strange gulping noises travelled along the phone. 'It tried to grab my-'

'Your what, Mr Swizzle?' As if I couldn't guess, Martin thought, dreading the reply.

Mr Swizzle coughed a few times. 'I don't want to discuss it, Mr Bramley. Suffice it to say that I'd be grateful if you'd pick up your keys from my office as soon as possible and take your business elsewhere. Good day to you, Mr Bramley.'

There was an angry click and the phone went dead.

***

Miserably, Martin ambled along the pavement, his hands stuck in his pockets, and he wondered what he was going to do. He couldn't get rid of the apartment and he couldn't take anyone home. Obviously there was no way that he could have a woman there to stay the night. She'd almost definitely be assaulted by a jealous Nancy! He was stuck with a possessive, oversexed, invisible mistress-

Who never belittled him or called him Darling, who never got drunk and laughed with a loud, horsy, bellowing laugh, who never refused sex because she'd just changed the sheets, who didn't spend a fortune on designer clothes that she only wore once, who didn't criticise his casual, comfortable clothes, and who couldn't stop him going out with his friends.

Martin's pace quickened and he began to swing his arms.

-Who didn't choose the dreadful dreary décor in the home, who didn't cook him meals that he couldn't stand because 'They're good for you darling, and you're beginning to put on weight,' who didn't count the number of whiskies that he drank after work, and who didn't change the 'Rubbish' that he was enjoying watching on the TV to 'Something more cultural, darling.'

Martin's walk became quite bouncy and he started to hum a tune. What was he complaining about? He'd got a dumb, invisible nymphomaniac – the perfect mistress!

He closed his front door behind him and leaned against it, surveying the mess with horror. Chairs lay on their side and his books were thrown around the room. At least she hadn't touched his whisky!

Crunching on eggshells, he marched into the bedroom. He sat on the edge of the bed and spoke out loud.

'OK Nancy, I want to talk to you. I know you can hear me, so you'd better listen carefully. I'll stay here with you as I don't seem to have any choice. But there are going to be a few changes around here. Sure, I love sex as much as the next man, and maybe more. But when I say No, I mean it. And if you get too pushy, I'll book into a hotel for a few nights.' He paused and listened, but there was just silence.

'Sometimes after work, I like to go out for a drink. And if I want to bring some of my friends home for a few beers, I will. And if I do, I don't want you hurling missiles at them. I'll decide who comes into my home. I'm the one who's paying the bills.'

So what had awakened Nancy? Had the builders disturbed her? Or was Martin the double of her lost lover? Maybe he'd do some research. But meanwhile, he had to control her. 'Looking at the state of the place, you're obviously capable of moving things around,' he continued, 'So there's nothing to stop you doing a bit of tidying up while I'm at work instead of just hovering around all day. Understand? And if you don't behave yourself, I'll have you exorcised. So watch it!'

Martin paused and listened. There wasn't a sound in the room. Nothing stirred, and the temperature stayed the same. But he knew instinctively that she'd heard him. With a smile, he undressed and climbed into bed.

Ogan the Chosen One

Keran Bluefield paused on her way to work.

She stared at the poster on the wall. It said,

Ladies, Ogan the Chosen One is coming to visit YOU!

Learn your Destiny. Tomorrow night! One night only. The Madeira Theatre.

Ladies aged 18-34.

Underneath was a coloured circle. As Keran stared at it, it seemed to start spinning, changing colour.

Must be a sort of hologram, she thought, An optical illusion. Then she shrugged and walked away.

In the workshop, everyone was talking about the posters, which apparently had appeared all over the town.

'I'd love to find out my destiny,' Anithia called out, bending over her machine. She had to talk loud to be heard over the rattling machines. 'I've been going out with Morgan for four years now, and there's no sign of him wanting to get married!'

'It's a load of rubbish,' Keran snorted, 'And why only women aged between 18 and 34?'

'That's probably where his powers work best,' Tishia said, 'And the theatre always recommends what ages their shows are suitable for. They can't allow children into a rude comedian, for instance.'

'Well I'm going for a laugh,' Anithia shouted, 'I want to know what he says about me.'

'I don't particularly want to know my destiny. It might be bad,' Keran muttered, concentrating on threading a needle on her machine.

I'm going to the theatre early to make sure I get a ticket before work tomorrow,' Keran's sister Jantice announced.

'I doubt if there'll be a queue,' Keran remarked cynically, 'And I certainly won't be there!'

'Oh come on Keran,' one of the group urged, 'It'll be really interesting. And we can all go for a drink afterwards.'

Keran shook her head. 'I honestly don't want to. I'm not feeling too good either. I think I'm going down with a cold or flu or something.'

'No wonder she's been so grumpy lately!' Anithia shouted to everyone. They all laughed, but in good humour. They were all friends.

***

Something woke Keran in the night – or she thought she was awake.

The room was freezing cold. Then she saw someone or something across her bedroom beside the door, slowly floating towards her bed.

She seemed to be paralysed. She couldn't even move her arms.

As it drew nearer, she silently gasped. It was the most gorgeous, handsome, perfect man that she'd ever seen in her life!

He sat down on her bed and she felt the mattress move. His wonderful bluey-green eyes stared deep into her eyes and the thought, I am Ogan, the Chosen One! filled her brain.

Gently, he brought his hand down and held it just above her right breast without touching her.

Her eyes were locked onto his, and her body completely filled with excitement until she thought it would never stop, and she climaxed effortlessly, shaking with passion for what seemed like ages.

Ogan smiled at her, then he seemed to float backwards, and vanished.

Keran lay there, filled with the most delicious feeling of release that she'd ever felt in her life. She'd had a few casual boyfriends, but she'd never experienced a feeling like this, or anywhere near it.

Totally relaxed, she dropped off to sleep. Or was she asleep all the time?

***

The front door slammed and Jantice rushed into the kitchen where her parents and Keran were having breakfast. Her large frame was shaking and she was out of breath.

'Look, I got the last two tickets!' she announced, waving them in the air. 'They're near the back and to the side, where there are pillars and the view isn't very good. But some people had been queuing since 5am, and the queue went right round the block. There were a lot of disappointed ladies behind me! And guess what, they were free! And look…' She held the silver tickets in her hand, then she scrunched them up and opened her hand again. Immediately, the tickets sprung back into shape again. 'Voila. Magic!'

Keran pushed her empty plate away and stood up. 'Magic, my backside. And I'm sure the Great Ogan will perform lots of 'magical' predictions tonight. I'm off to work.'

'Here's your ticket, Keran,' Jantice said, 'I'll meet you there this evening.'

'I'll see, but I doubt it,' Keran called back over her shoulder, taking the ticket.

***

Everyone in the workshop had managed to get tickets and they were all talking about the show.

Keran took her ticket out of her bag and glanced at it. There was the same coloured circle on it as on the poster and it seemed to spin as Keran looked at it.

'I had the most amazing dream,' Anithia shouted, 'I dreamt that Ogan appeared in my bedroom, and, ooh he was GORGEOUS!

Suddenly all work ceased. 'I had that dream!' Tishia gasped, 'And, wow, it had the most wonderful ending!' She swivelled her hips and laughed and a ripple of movement went around the room. Some of the women bent over their sewing, obviously embarrassed, and others looked up, amazed.

'I had that dream!' someone called out, gradually followed by everyone else.

'It must be some kind of hallucination,' Keran said, 'Go on then Anithia, tell us what he was wearing.'

'He had shoulder-length blonde hair, gorgeous bluey-green eyes, and he was wearing a deep blue tunic top and black trousers.'

Everyone murmured in agreement as Anithia spoke.

'I'm really looking forward to this evening. It should be amazing,' declared Tishia. Everyone nodded, agreeing with her.

'Well I won't be there,' Keran said, 'I'm definitely going down with a rotten fluey cold. It's been hovering for the past few days. I'll be in bed early with a hot drink.'

***

'I wish I hadn't come. I feel dreadful.' Keran blew into a handful of tissues.

'Oh stop moaning. Once the show starts you'll forget about your cold. If Ogan really looks like he did in my dream…' Jantice paused and actually blushed as she relived her dream… 'We'll all be so enthralled that we'll be concentrating on him.'

'Yeah, I can hardly wait. I'm sure he'll play every dirty trick in the book. And I wish this pillar wasn't in the way. I can only see half the stage unless I lean towards you.'

Gradually the lights went out and some strange, hypnotic music filled the theatre. There was complete silence. Then two men, both as gorgeous as Ogan, walked on from behind the curtain and stood, one at each side of the stage, standing with their arms folded and their legs astride. All the women leaned forward, tense and waiting.

Suddenly, Ogan appeared in the centre of the stage. Keran was certain that the curtains hadn't moved.

He raised his arms and boomed, 'I am Ogan, the Chosen One.'

The two assistants started chanting and quietly and in unison, all the women began chanting,

We're following Ogan,
Ogan the chosen One.
We're following Ogan,
We are the Chosen Ones.

Ogan lowered and raised his arms, encouraging them to chant louder. The volume gradually increased.

Keran muffled a sneeze in her tissues and looked at her sister. Her eyes were glazed and she stared blankly ahead while she chanted.

A huge attack of sneezing and sniffles forced Keran to bury her face in her tissues and her ears blocked up. She stuck out her tongue and wiggled it from side to side and cleared her ears.

But what was that horrible noise?

Keran looked at the stage and blinked her eyes. She looked away and back again. No it was still there. The gorgeous Ogan had turned into a giant lizard-like creature! Both of his assistants were also lizard people. And oh, the terrible tuneless noise they were making. It was unbearable! There were no words; it was just a din.

Was one of the assistants looking directly at her? Keran turned her head to look at Ogan and leaned sideways behind the pillar, out of view, forcing herself to chant over the dreadful din. She glanced back. No, the lizard thing wasn't looking at her any more.

Then the lights came on, but the chanting increased. The lizard Ogan held his stumpy arms out and all the women stood up. Keran looked sideways at Jantice, who effortlessly rose to her feet, although she usually had to push herself up using her arms. She was completely unaware of Keran beside her.

Ogan turned his scaly back and led the way off the side of the stage, his long tail swinging behind him, followed by his assistants.

Starting at the front row, the women followed him up the steps onto the stage and behind the curtain, one by one. They all still chanted as they happily marched along.

Jantice and Keran were in the third to back row, and when it was finally their turn, Jantice blankly pushed Keran forward with her stomach.

Keran marched along, chanting, but when she was finally up on the stage, she darted sideways and buried herself in the folds of the curtain. Nobody noticed and they continued their hypnotised trek.

She remained quiet and still until the chanting women had obviously all passed her. Then she peeped out in the direction of the departing women.

One of the lizard assistants was standing by the fire exit door and Keran could see the women marching across the car park towards a huge object in the playing field beyond. They marched up a ramp and into the strange object.

The lizard followed them up the ramp and the door started to shut.

Oh no, it can't be! Keran thought, It's a UFO! They're kidnapping all the women!

Keran ran quietly along the aisle, through the double doors and down the stairs into the foyer. And then she began to scream for help.

She saw Mr Fulmore, the theatre manager, but he was sitting on the floor with his back against the ticket office, his knees drawn up with his arms folded across them and his head resting on them. He was snoring quietly.

'Mr Fulmore! Mr Fulmore!' she cried, shaking his shoulder. Mr Fulmore fell gently sideways and laid snoring on the ground.

Now full of panic, Keran ran towards the front doors and tugged at them, but they didn't open. She tugged her way along the row and found a green button that opened the last door.

Relieved, she burst into the street, screaming 'Help!' And she noticed that something was wrong. The street was empty. There were no people and no cars. Nothing.

On the other side of the road, the Theatre Inn was lit up. She ran across the road and pulled open the door. And paused. All the customers were asleep. Some of them were resting on their arms on the table, some sat upright with their heads dropped forwards, and the men sitting on bar stools leaned on an arm on the bar.

'Wake up!' she screamed, 'Oh, wake up will you? It's an emergency!'

Everyone carried on sleeping. Keran looked around her desperately, and saw the big bell hanging behind the bar to call Last Orders.

She went behind the bar and rang the bell, shouting, 'Wake up everyone! Will you wake up?'

It worked. As one the customers regained consciousness, and carried on drinking and talking, obviously unaware of what had happened to them.

'Will you all shut up and listen?' Keran called as loudly as she could, ringing the bell again.

'Hello young Keran, where did you spring from?' asked Old Will, the newsagent.

Keran shook her hands in the air. 'You've got to come quick. All the girls are being kidnapped by aliens that look like lizards! They've followed him into a huge UFO. Please come!'

There was a ripple of laughter. 'Are you sure it's not the Pied Piper?' asked one of the men sitting at the bar.

Walking towards him, Keran screamed, 'No it's NOT the Pied bloody Piper! And what do you care anyway, Morgan, if Anithia's abducted? You never loved her anyway!'

Morgan stopped laughing. 'I love Anithia very much. Are you sure this isn't a joke, Keran?'

Keran placed her hands over her eyes. 'Will you all please believe me?' They've abducted everyone out of the theatre.' Then she realised something and said, 'Check your watches. Go on, check them and see how much time you've lost while you were asleep!'

All the men looked at their watches and began to realise that they were missing over an hour.

'Perhaps they were terrorists,' one of them said, 'They must have squirted some sort of gas in here to make us unconscious. I read once about a group of girls that were kidnapped from their school.'

'Yes, I read that,' said someone else.

Morgan got down off his stool and started for the door. Someone call the police,' he said, 'I'm going to look for my Anithia!'

'Right, I'm coming to find out what's going on,' said the local PC, Niall Webb, taking a final swig of his brown ale and slamming the glass down on the table.

'Will you please hurry before it's too late!' Keran pleaded, running down the road, followed by everyone from the Theatre Inn. She turned left into the theatre car park. And she paused, pointing upwards. 'We're too late,' she sobbed, 'They've gone!'

The UFO had already risen into high the air and it shot rapidly sideways and disappeared.

Afterwards, the witnesses said they'd seen everything from a UFO to a shooting star.

PC Webb decided to take control. 'Where did you see this – thing – parked?' he asked.

Keran pointed. 'In the field. Over there.'

'OK, stand back everyone,' PC Webb ordered. He took out his phone and turned on the light. Bending down, he inspected the ground. 'There's an indentation in the ground,' he said at once.

'And there are two near each other,' Morgan called.

'That's where the ramp went up,' Keran told the men.

Everyone was talking at once, but they went quiet as Dick Colborn the barman called, 'Come and see this! Quick, everyone!'

'What's up, Dick? You look as though you've seen a ghost,' PC Webb called. Standing in the light by the exit door, it was obvious that Dick was in a state of shock.

With Dick leading the way, all the men went into the theatre, and couldn't believe what they saw.

There were rows of handbags by the empty seats, with occasional jackets and pairs of shoes.

Mr Fulmore sat in a front seat, rocking to and fro, and repeating, 'It's not my fault. I fell asleep. It's not my fault. Where have they all gone?' He was still repeating it when the ambulance took him away.

'See, now do you believe me?' Keran demanded.

Near-panic was setting in as the men started checking the handbags, looking for their family members and girlfriends.

'Don't you move anything!' shouted the PC, 'It's all evidence.' Then he sat down on the front seat and beckoned Keran to sit next to him. 'Now tell me exactly what happened, young Keran,' he said.

Keran briefly repeated the events of the evening while PC Webb shook his head, partly unable to believe what he was hearing, but forced to believe what he could see.

'I'll need a full statement from you, Keran,' he said, 'But now I'm going to call for backup.'

'Can you take it in the morning?' Keran begged, standing up, 'I've got to go home and tell my parents that their daughter has been abducted by aliens, and it isn't going to be easy!'

***

Mrs Bluefield was bent over the oven with her oven gloves on, lifting out a casserole dish. She had a strange expression on her face as she saw Keran. 'Hello luv,' she said, 'Sorry, dinner's a bit late. Your Dad and I felt a bit unwell-'

'We felt really tired and fell asleep-'

'On the kitchen floor,' uttered Mrs Bluefield. 'Where's Jantice?'

Keran went and placed her arm round her mother's shoulders. 'Sit down Mum, and you Dad. I've got to talk to you.'

***

The whole world became involved in the hunt for the 540 missing women, although most of the National press was no use at all as they tried to turn it into a semi-joke, writing ridiculous headlines about little green men.

All their names and photos were circulated which created thousands of calls, all of which had to be followed up.

One woman ran naked into a police station in America, claiming that she'd been raped by an alien. But the only one arrested was her drugs dealer.

***

The months passed and things changed in the town. Keran and Morgan got married, drawn together in their grief. Morgan started a successful career as a tour guide.

Dick Colburn the barman took over the lease of the Theatre Inn and changed its name to The Ogan.

Several souvenir shops popped up in the High Street, and a plaque was placed in the playing fields, which was regularly stolen by souvenir hunters and replaced.

Every time the story was revived the numbers of worldwide sightings increased. But none of the women were ever seen again. They had vanished for ever.

So had Ogan the Chosen One.

Stan and Stanley

'Two hundred grams of Vampire's Fangs please Mr Grimble.'

'Certainly young lady. Two hundred grams coming up.' Stan forced a smile as he weighed the gooey sweets, resting his thumb on the scales for good measure. He hated kids. They had too much money nowadays. And you had to watch them like a hawk.

'Bye-bye dear. See you soon. Give my regards to your parents.' He waved the little girl out of the shop and sighed. Ten minutes to closing time. And then what? Another evening in the back room watching the telly, alone and unloved. 'Thank you Mother,' he muttered, 'You stole my youth!'

He could go down to the pub for a quick pint, but it was always the same; sarky comments about when was he going to buy a round of drinks, or how were the moths in his wallet. Well he knew they didn't really like him very much so he wasn't going to waste his hard-earned money on them!

The bell tinkled as the door opened and Stan forced his money-making smile onto his plump face.

'Can I help-' he began. And froze.

'Yes, I was-' the customer began. And froze.

Stan stared, pop-eyed at – himself! His double stared back. They both had the same thinning hair with side parting, the same frown lines clustered above the nose, the same bulging paunch. Only the clothes were different. Stan wore a shabby, off-white overall, worn grey trousers and unpolished, scuffed black lace-up shoes. His doppelganger was expensively and immaculately clothed.

Two mouths slowly dropped open and two pairs of eyes travelled downwards while the men patted themselves, checking that they weren't dreaming. Then they pointed to each other and gurgled, 'You-you look just like me!'

Hurrying over to the front door, Stan locked it and turned the 'open' sign to 'closed' five minutes early for the first time in his life. He tried not to imagine the money that he might be losing.

'I think we could do with a drink,' he gasped.

'I think we could,' his double agreed.

They talked through the night, pouring out whisky and troubles. Stan Grimble was forty-seven. He opened the corner newsagent's seven days a week. He was the third generation of his family to run it. 'And the last,' he said bitterly, draining his whisky. He'd hardly ever been out of Tidfield in his life. He'd hardly ever been allowed out of range of his neurotic mother's voice.

Stanley Ashton was a year older. He was a Company Director with a big house, a flash car and an ulcer. He was on his way back from a meeting in Scotland and he'd become tired of the monotony of motorway driving so he'd turned off, searching for a country inn.

Stan's domineering mother had died last year, leaving him her life savings and an inbred bitterness. 'Stan! Stan!' she'd shrieked a million times a day from her armchair in the lounge. He often winced, thinking that he could still hear her.

Stanley's nagging, nit-picking, social-climbing wife was still alive and picking. 'Oh Stanley,' she'd sigh as though he was a tiresome child. She never called him Stan. She thought it was common.

'Do you know, I really envy you!' both Stans burst out simultaneously at 3am.

***

Unaccustomed to such a powerful machine, Stan Grimble drove the Aston Martin slowly along the road. Then he thought of Mrs Ashton; Maud, whose bed he would be sharing that night. His only experience of women had been imaginary while thumbing through the magazines from the top shelf in his newsagent's. And now he'd been given a wife to practise on!

Throwing back his head he laughed aloud, something that he hadn't done since he was a child. 'Goodbye Mother!' he shouted, 'and look out Maud, here I come!'

Pressing down firmly on the accelerator he roared out of Tidfield for ever.

***

Grinning, Stanley Ashton watched his leased vehicle disappear out of his life.

'I'm free!' he announced to the deserted street.

He pictured an eager Stan trying to snuggle up to his wife that night and being angrily rebuffed. Or maybe he'd manage to melt the frigid bitch somehow? Well, good luck to him. He was welcome. And she'd never notice that her husband had changed. She'd never taken any notice of the original version!

Oh what he'd give to see her face if she ever found out that she was sleeping with a total stranger! But no, she must never find out.

The shop next door caught his eye. It was empty. A For Sale sign was propped carelessly inside the dusty window. That would make a perfect café, Stanley thought. He could fill it with a pool table, a football game and fruit machines. The local kids never have anywhere to hang out in small towns like Tidfield.

Stanley liked kids. They had money to spend. And on market days he'd do a roaring trade. Nothing fancy or Cordon Bleu, just bacon butties, hotpot, coffee and things like that.

He had to buy some new clothes. Stan obviously hadn't bought any clothes for years. And he needed a decent car. The Morris Minor in the garage was a collector's item. It had hardly been used. The mileage was lower than Stanley's

Aston Martin, which was less than a year old! And the house behind the shop was badly in need of modernising. And… No! Slow down, Stanley, he silently ordered.

Obviously Stan and his mother had been great hoarders. Luckily they'd hoarded every penny. Stan's bank account was very healthy indeed! Stanley thought of his permanent overdraft and he shuddered. No more, he reminded himself, and I'm Stan now, not Stanley.

He had a new signature to practise. And he had to take great care until he was settled and he'd got to know people. Mustn't give himself away! And he wouldn't have any big money-making plans. He was rid of ambition for ever! The money was going to stay where it was now; safely in the bank. He wasn't going to touch it. In fact he was going to add to it, as Stan had done. Well, perhaps a few new clothes wouldn't break the bank. After all, he was an eligible batchelor now!

Closing his eyes he breathed deeply, savouring the smells around him.

Two girls clattered along the pavement, wobbling on their high heels. Stan eyed them warily. Would they suspect anything?

'Morning Mr Grimble!' they trilled.

'Morning ladies,' Stanley Ashton replied, ogling their legs.

'You seem in a good mood,' one of them commented.

'For once,' muttered her friend. They both giggled.

Stanley grinned. He'd passed the inaugural test. 'Yes,' he agreed, 'Today's the first day of the rest of my life. And I feel like a new man!'

***

Cocooned in the car and engrossed in the music that surrounded him, Stan Grimble opened his mouth wide, singing loudly and tunelessly. He hadn't had much practice. His mother had disapproved of singing.

He leaned back in the leather seat and gripped the steering-wheel. He'd hardly ever been in a car on his own before. His mother had always sat upright in the back, calling, 'Slow down, Stan. You're not on a racetrack!' if he went over 30mph. Oh this was the life! He couldn't remember such a feeling of exhilaration!

All he had to do was nod and agree in the right places. It was home – his new home – with Maud waiting for him!

'Yippee!' he cried, not noticing the lorry cutting in front of him. He didn't stand a chance.

***

Maud identified her husband's body. The idiot was probably driving far too fast as usual, she was sure. Luckily the insurance would make her a rich widow, so she had generously decided to forgive Stanley's last act of stupidity.

As she walked away from the corpse she couldn't help thinking that there had been something different about her husband's appearance, but she was unable to pinpoint exactly what it was. Perhaps it was the strange enigmatic little smile curling up the corners of his mouth?

A Head of His Time

'Gadzooks, I'm tired!' muttered Sir Percy, pausing beside a garden seat, 'And I've got the devil of a headache!'

He slowly lowered himself onto the bench and carefully placed his head beside him.

It was a quiet area of the estate, tucked behind where the kitchens were. Not many members of the public bothered to walk around here.

Gazing critically at the leaves and the litter blowing across the elaborate gardens, his head let out a sigh. They don't train gardeners like they used to, he thought. They'd have been stuck in the pillory for a few days if they'd neglected their work like this lot do! Then he winced as two boys dashed across the flower-bed, yelling, 'Oy Mum, over 'ere!' and 'Cor, look at that 'ouse! Wicked, innit?' One of them threw an empty sandwich carton on the lawn.

'What have they done to our beautiful language?' Sir Percy pondered, 'It used to be a joy to listen to, but nowadays the harsh sounds rattle around inside the skull like a musket ball!'

He rested his hand on the head beside him protectively. Then he spotted the children's mother, who was acting very strangely.

She was furtively looking around her, checking that nobody was watching.

Sir Percy raised his head by the hair so that he could have a clearer view. Then he gasped as the woman bent down and pulled up some of the carefully-arranged plants and stuck them in her bag.

'Damn and blast your eyes, Madame!' Sir Percy bellowed, but the woman couldn't hear him.

He slumped back on the seat, letting his head drop, his thoughts confused. What was happening to the human race? They tore up his plants, they galloped all over the garden, they wrote strange patterns on his walls; they didn't have any respect for anything! Why did they bother coming here if they didn't feel any love for it?

The stonemasons had laboured for years, designing and building Sir Percy's new home. They'd been proud of their work, overseeing every carefully-carved stone as it was hauled up by ropes and cemented into place. And people had travelled for miles to see the expensive leaded glass in the windows.

Even the staff didn't bother to look after their things any more.

Sir Percy had watched a gardener that morning, hacking away at the branch of a tree with a blunt axe. The job would have been much quicker and easier if the man had spent a little time honing it first. No idea, any of them! He patted his head again. Now there was a man who'd looked after his tools! What was the executioner's name? De Wolfe, or something like that. Sir Percy's memory was getting weaker as the centuries passed. Aah, what a man! He'd never needed more than one stroke to separate a head from its body!

With a shiver, Sir Percy recalled the day when he'd been led, bound and blindfolded, up the steps towards the executioner's block. Those final memories never faded. It was as clear as the day that it had happened. He could hear the murmuring of the crowd. His legs had been shaking so much that it had taken two strong men to hold him up. They'd forced him onto his knees with his head over the edge of the wooden block. And then – boff! It was all over! He'd hardly felt a thing!

Chuckling, Sir Percy reached down to his head and gently re-arranged his hair. His only crime had been to get caught praying on the losing side. They'd kept on changing the religion and he'd foolishly thought that he was ahead of the game. He'd been sure that he'd picked the next winner. But he was mistaken, so he'd lost his head. And what did it matter anyway? They'd all got it wrong.

Now here he was stuck in a time warp, condemned to watch his lovely home turned into a museum, regularly vandalised in front of his eyes. It was a tragedy.

The two boys tore past him, shouting and fighting and kicking at the shrubs. Their mother trailed behind, yelling at them. They both ignored her and ran towards where Sir Percy was seated.

Feeling some of his old spirit return, Sir Percy grasped his head and stood up, concentrating hard.

He breathed in and, shaking his head in front of him, he yelled, 'Boo!'

Simultaneously braking to a standstill, the boys stared. All the colour drained out of their faces until they were nearly as pale as Sir Percy. Flinging their arms round each other, they began to tremble violently.

Their mother had stopped behind them. She was unsure of what she'd seen. But looking at the state of her sons, she was pretty sure that they'd seen the same thing. An old man in a funny outfit. And his head seemed to be moving around, separate from his body!

The boys began to slowly walk backwards. Their legs wouldn't function properly. Then they turned and dashed away, crying, 'Muuuum!'

'Justin! Jason!' come 'ere!' yowled their mum, grabbing their arms and rushing away, dragging them along. She paused to glance back over her shoulder, then she ran towards the car park.

Waving his head around, Sir Percy laughed till his sides ached. 'Ooh, I enjoyed that!' he chuckled, gasping for breath. Then he stopped, feeling tired and worn out. It was time for his afternoon rest. Maybe one day he wouldn't wake up here.

Maybe it would be time for him to move on to another place. He hoped so. He was tired of existing like he did day after day; year after year; century after long century. His body ached and walking through walls was an effort now. Sometimes he got stuck, halfway through.

Slowly he shuffled along the uneven path towards his castle. Aah, they don't make garden paths like they used to, he mused, cradling his head under his arm and gently pinching himself on the cheek. 'Come on, head,' he said, 'Maybe you and I will be joined together again one day soon.'

Dining Out

'I don't want to go out tonight, Karl.'

Catherine's husband looked at her, his face full of concern. 'What's the matter, old girl? Feeling a bit off colour?'

She smiled at him. 'No, I'm fine, dear. But we shouldn't keep on going out night after night. It's not right.'

'Why not? We worked hard all our lives and never received any thanks from anyone. So why shouldn't we enjoy ourselves now? We deserve it.'

'Yes,' she agreed, 'But – well, supposing something happened – something unexpected? What would we do, Karl?'

'Now there you go, worrying about nothing again,' he soothed, 'What could possibly happen? And we've always got this lovely big house to fall back on, haven't we?'

Catherine nodded. 'I know. But it would be nice to have something at home for a change.'

'It's such a lot of bother though, isn't it? And I'm only thinking of what's best for you, my dear.' Karl smiled lovingly at his wife.

She sighed. 'I suppose you're right. But I would like to have an evening at home, just the two of us. And I've overdone it a bit lately, so I'm going on a diet.'

'You don't need to diet, Catherine my love. You've got a beautiful figure.' And he meant it. He thought that his wife was lovely.

'Ooh, you old flatterer, you!' giggled Catherine. She examined her husband. In all their years together, they'd never had a cross word between them. Karl's head of hair was still black and wavy, his body slim and upright.

What a lucky woman I am, Catherine thought to herself.

'Alright,' Karl decided, 'If you really want to stay in, we will. You know I'd do anything for you, old girl.'

As the evening passed, Karl began to drum his fingers, then he got up and paced about, humming a tune.

Catherine knew that he didn't want to stay in. He'd become used to his nights out.

'Why don't you go out, Karl?' she suggested gently.

He stopped his pacing.'Go out without you? No, I wouldn't dream of it, my dear!'

'Oh go on, be off with you!' she urged.

'Well if you're sure you don't mind,' he said, 'And you won't sit up worrying about me.'

'Worry about you? Why should I worry about you, you silly old fool?' Catherine joked.

Karl rubbed his hands together. 'I might meet some young, nubile maiden who'll be unable to resist me!'

Catherine laughed. 'No young, nubile maiden's going to notice you!'

'Alright then, I'll go. I know when I'm not wanted!' Karl headed for the door, then he paused. 'Promise me that you won't wait up for me.'

'I promise,' she agreed, 'In fact I thought I'd have an early night for a change.'

'Goodbye then, my dear.' And he'd gone.

As soon as he'd left, Catherine changed her mind. She didn't want to stay in on her own after all. The house felt cold and empty without his presence, and she was beginning to feel hungry.

She hurried after him as fast as she could. But she didn't need to call him. They had been together for so long that they could usually anticipate each other's thoughts. Karl was waiting for her and his face lit up when she appeared.

'Oh, I'm so glad you've come, my dear!' he cried, 'Where would you like to go tonight? The choice is entirely yours.'

Catherine cocked her head on one side. 'Somewhere small and peaceful.'

'Just what I was thinking,' he agreed.

They stopped outside a window and peeped in.

'I say,' Karl whispered, 'She's a tasty young thing!'

'Now you behave yourself, you old devil, you!' Catherine threatened in mock anger, 'Ooh, her young man's rather dishy too!'

Karl pretended to frown at her. 'Catherine, I'm ashamed of you, a woman of your mature years!'

Suddenly Catherine felt very tired. Pangs of hunger gnawed at her stomach. She heard Karl's voice saying, 'Shall we go in or not?' and she nodded weakly. She hadn't the strength to go any further.

Together, they flew through the open window, landing lightly, one each side of the bed.

I'll start my diet tomorrow, Catherine vowed to herself. Then she bent down and sank her teeth in the sleeping man's neck.

Jealous Earth

The inn was perfect. It seemed to be everything that an English country pub should be, lop-sided with Tudor beams and ivy clinging confidently to the walls. All the windows were lit up with a warm, pinkish glow, inviting passers-by to hurry inside, out of the cold, damp air.

Jilly Acton switched off her engine and sighed with relief. She'd been twisting and winding along narrow country lanes for ages, straining her eyes to see anything through the horrible rainy drizzle. She was beginning to feel tired with a bit of a headache, and quite worried when she finally spotted the distant lights of the pub, twinkling through the mist.

She opened the wooden front door and was immediately enveloped in a welcoming warmth. A huge log fire crackled and spat in an old inglenook fireplace, horse brasses covered all the beams, and pictures of hunting scenes hung on the walls. Perfect. A tourist's dream of old England, thought Jilly, smiling to herself.

Two old men sat at a table playing dominoes, and a middle-aged couple perched side by side on the window seat. They all acknowledged her with warm smiles, then they carried on with their own conversations.

'Rotten night to be out driving,' the landlord said in a friendly voice.

'Yes, it's awful.' Jilly climbed onto an old leather-covered bar stool. 'A brandy and ginger please,' she ordered, 'And do you have a room for the night?'

'We certainly have.' The landlord placed the drink on a beermat in front of her. 'Go and get your luggage and Norma my wife will show you upstairs. By the way, my name's Bill.'

'My name's Jilly,' she said. Then she obediently dashed outside in the cold and grabbed her case out of the boot, and followed the landlord's wife up the creaky wooden stairs to the room.

'Alright?' Bill inquired when she returned to the bar.

Jilly nodded. It was lovely and just what she'd expected; an old brass bed, a dark red rug on the polished wooden floor, and an oak wardrobe with a creaky door.

Another door led to a small bathroom.

'So what brings a young lady like you way out here on a night like this?' Bill asked, wiping the bar with a cloth.

'I'm on holiday,' Jilly told him, 'I seem to have spent most of my life studying, so I'm having a six months' break before I start work. My parents think it's a great idea and they've given me the money. I'm touring England, just pointing my car and going where I want to. It's really interesting. And I'm collecting unusual stories as I travel. I hope to get them published – that's if I write them well enough!'

'Unusual stories, eh?' Bill rested his hand on his cloth and stared at her for a few seconds. He seemed to be sizing her up. Then he gave a slight nod, as though she'd passed his approval.

He indicated towards the fireplace with his cloth. 'If you want to hear an unusual story, you go and talk to Dan Randall over there.'

Jilly looked over to where he pointed, and was surprised to see a man seated in the inglenook. She hadn't noticed him before. He was rather nice-looking too! He seemed to be around her own age, 25, or he may have been nearer 30. It was hard to tell. A farmer, Jilly guessed, by his weather-beaten face and his old clothes.

Picking up her drink, she walked over to the fireplace and stood in front of the man. He didn't look up, although Jilly knew instinctively that he was aware of her presence. She felt a twinge of disappointment. She was used to men's admiring glances. But he just sat, hunched forwards, with both hands cupped around his pint glass, staring into the fire. The reflection of the dancing flames cast a strange, devilish glow on his face.

Jilly swallowed nervously, wondering if she should walk back to the bar. She forced herself to speak. 'Hello, I'm-'

'I know,' the man interrupted, 'I heard.' His voice wasn't friendly, but it wasn't unfriendly either. It was as though he had far more important things to think about than Jilly.

Unsure of what to do next, Jilly was about to turn and leave him when he stared up at her. 'It's unusual stories you want, is it?' he asked. Jilly nodded eagerly. 'Well sit down then.' He flapped a hand towards the seat on the other side of the fire and Jilly obediently sat down.

'I'll tell you a story that's as unusual as can be,' the man continued, 'But I'm not playing questions and answers. I'll tell it and I'll tell it my way, and I don't want any interruptions.'

Jilly shook her head, silently promising to keep quiet.

As the man told his tale, the mental questions piled up in her brain. He had a strange accent that she couldn't pinpoint, and he used some quaint expressions. But Jilly was a sensible girl and her training as a solicitor had made her a good listener. So she kept her word and remained silent while he spoke.

'My parents had a farm which they ran on their own without any help, except from me. It's not very big, but they grew lovely fruit and vegetables, herbs and flowers, the best for miles around, or maybe further. And their animals never suffered with any ailments.

'Mother was what you'd call a white witch, 'cept there's no such thing.' His expression softened and he half-smiled to himself. 'In those days people were more aware of Mother Earth's amazing powers.'

In those days? thought Jilly, feeling disappointed. So Dan Randall was the village story teller, and she wasn't going to hear anything to add to her collection.

Actually, a good storyteller was a dying art, so maybe the fact that Dan Randall was one of a surviving few was a story in itself!

Well, it was a lousy night and he made the story sound interesting, so she may as well sit and listen.

'Nowadays,' Dan continued, 'People plug things in and press buttons, and they think they're clever and civilised. But they're not. They've forgotten that the Earth is a living thing. They've lost the mental and physical link between them and the trees, the streams and the soil. Their feet hardly ever touch the ground, so they don't feel the throbbing of life through their toes. They swallow medicines and tablets, and they've no idea what the ingredients are, or what harm they can do. They start up their noisy, air-destroying cars and point them at where they want to go, while they just sit there. They don't share the love and togetherness between them and a loyal horse, and Mother Earth.'

Dan sighed and sipped his beer. Jilly thought what a marvellous narrator he was. He even acted out the part! She wondered if it was a natural talent, or whether he'd had any drama training.

'My Mother was even closer to Nature than most. She knew the best plants to pick for her potions. And she only had to lay her hands on folk to cure all kinds of ailments.

'Funny though, for all her knowledge, she'd never had any children. Her and Dad tried all the cures and remedies going which worked on other folk, but they didn't work on my parents. But they were in love and they never blamed each other. And in the end, they said it just wasn't meant to be, and they gave it up as a bad job and just got on with their life.

'Imagine their surprise and joy then when they found out that I was on the way! At first they couldn't believe it and thought that it was Mother Nature playing one of her little tricks, or my mother's Change starting. And when they were sure about it, they decided that I was going to be the most loved and best looked-after child that ever there was born.

'But I was in no hurry to be born. My Mother lay tossing and turning in labour for three full days and nights. And when I finally entered this world, they said you could hear her screams right through the village. The midwife said it was the hardest labour she'd ever seen. My Mother was forty-eight years old!

'They did their best for my Mother. The doctor called in twice a day. They said her face lit up lovely every time I was placed in her arms. But the birth had taken its toll. She died five days later of childbed fever.

'My Dad thought the world of me, but he didn't spoil me. He taught me right from wrong, and gave me a good hiding whenever I deserved it, which was as often as any growing lad.

'As soon as I was old enough, I worked with Dad on the farm. I seemed to have inherited some of Mother's talents because the plants grew eagerly under my hands. I worked hard, but I had a happy childhood and lots of free time to play with all my friends. It's true what they say; the Summers used to last longer in the old days.'

His little half-smile appeared and lit up his face as he gazed into the crackling log fire. Jilly couldn't take her eyes off him. She hung on to every word he said.

'Things were fine till I was twelve. A Mayday fair had come to the next village and we were all eager to go. We'd had fairs in our village of course, but none so grand as that one. Go on, said my Dad, There's nothing here for you to do that won't keep for another day.

'So I got up at daybreak to give my Dad a hand with the milking, then I set out with my friends to walk the eight miles or so to the next village.

'We travelled along, turning the journey into an adventure as children do, chasing each other, pulling the girls' hair until they squealed, and whacking stones along the road with sticks. One boy was real talented at holding a blade of grass between his thumbs and playing a tune, so we had a merry sing-song to help us on our way.

'Eventually we reached what you'd class as the edge of our village. We could see the rooftops and the church spire of the next village in the distance. We all started to run down the hill, and that's when it happened. I got an attack of stomach cramps something rotten. Doubled up with pain, I shouted to my friends to wait and they all came running back, concerned about me. We decided that I'd probably got a stitch and I'd be alright in a few minutes, so they sat down with me and ate most of their picnics while they waited.

'But I didn't get any better and they were anxious to be on their way, so I told them to go without me, then I turned and headed for home, with my arm wrapped around my stomach, fighting back my tears of pain and disappointment. And then my pains vanished as quick as they'd come. Relieved, I hollered to my friends and ran after them. And back came my pains!

'Three times that happened, and then I gave up. And once again, as I headed for home, the pains disappeared without a trace of them ever having been there at all. Real strange it was. And real upset I was, I can tell you.

'The doctor examined me, thinking it might be my appendix. But the pains had completely gone.

'Life carried on as it usually did until I was eighteen. Then I fell in love with Caroline, and she fell in love with me. We'd known each other all our lives and I'd pulled her hair a few times, and she'd kicked me on the shin a few times. Then suddenly one day I noticed how beautiful she'd become.

'Everyone knew that we were courting. We walked through the village hand-in-hand, and she'd come and talk to me at the farm while I was working. My Dad said he'd be glad when we got married because the plants were suffering. And they didn't seem to be in as good condition as they usually were, it was true enough.

'Once, when the weather was bad, we were sitting in Caroline's front parlour on the sofa. Bold as brass, I put my arm round her and kissed her on the cheek. She blushed and giggled, and her Mum rushed in and glared at us. Then I blushed too, I can tell you!

'When I asked her to marry me and she said yes, I thought I was the luckiest man alive! Caroline's parents and my Dad were happy too, which was good, and suddenly we were left alone more.

'I remember the day it happened as though it was yesterday. A fine hot summer's day it was. Caroline and I were wandering hand-in-hand over the hills. Then she said something silly to me and ran away with me chasing her. We both knew the hills like the back of our hands, or maybe better, so I wasn't bothered when Caroline ran along the bank of the Yellowbourne stream. It was a steep bank and a long drop to the tiny stream below, but there were lots of footholds on the way down, and we'd run up and down every one of them, I should think.

'Suddenly, Caroline looked back at me and her lovely laughing face changed to an expression of horror. She didn't just fall; she seemed to be lifted and thrown through the air!

'She screamed and disappeared over the edge. I screamed too, shouting her name and running towards her. I leaped over the bank and I could see her lying face down in the stream. But I never reached her. A tree root wrapped itself round my ankle and held me tight. And I watched helplessly as my darling Caroline drowned in the stream.'

'But you said it was a lovely day,' Jilly interrupted, 'Was the stream flooded?'

Dan shook his head. He didn't seem to resent her interruption. 'She drowned in three inches of water.'

Jilly gasped. Then she realised that it was just a story.

Taking a sip of his beer, Dan continued. 'They came searching for us at sunset. They had to go back to the village to get a saw to set me free. The tree root was wrapped round my ankle three times, stopping me from falling down the bank.

'They carried me back home and I lay in my bed in shock and with a high fever for six weeks. Then I just sat around moping for a couple of months. But funny enough, my plants all bucked up and thrived.

'The doctor suggested that I ought to go away and convalesce for a while, so Dad wrote to a cousin of his who lived on the coast. He wrote back and said that he and his wife would be pleased to put me up for as long as I wanted to stay with them, and that the sea air would do me good.

'So off I set on one of our horses until we reached the edge of the village. And that horse wouldn't go no further for begs nor beating! I took my belongings off his back and sent him home. He trotted away, happy as can be and I set off on foot. But I only managed to go a short way before the stomach cramps attacked me, and I knew it was hopeless. There was no way that the village would let me go.'

'Let you go?' Jilly exclaimed.

Dan looked at her for several seconds across the small table before he continued speaking. 'Haven't you realised?' he asked, 'Before my Mother died, she dedicated me to Mother Earth, the most jealous, possessive Mother that any son could ever have. She won't let me have a life of my own, but she won't let me die either. I've been doomed to stay in this village under her constant protection. I've never been ill and I've never got any older than I am now.'

'Can I ask you something please?' Jilly inquired softly. He nodded slightly and she knew that he'd anticipated her question. He's probably heard it many times before. 'How old are you?'

He sighed. 'I'll be two hundred next month.'

'Two hundred?' Jilly burst out, laughing instinctively. But the laughter died on her lips as she stared into his eyes and beyond, back, back through the centuries. And she knew that his story was true.

She spoke again, in a respectful whisper. 'How have you spent your time?'

'On my farm mostly. Word soon spread through the village, as word usually does, that strange things often happened to folk who became too close to me. Parents forbade their daughters from going out with me, and although my friends still passed the time of day with me, they didn't want to hang around with me any more. And who could blame them?

'Through the years the village has looked after me and protected me from the outside world. They all know my story. I'm surrounded by kind, helpful people, but I'm lonely as can be. Trapped in a cage of kindness.

'My old friends have all died long ago, of course, but my plants still live and my farm does well. I never sell anything though. I give things away to folk. Funny though, I can't give anything away to anyone out of the village. The plants will die, and any meat or veg makes them ill. Sometimes I exchange things locally for clothes or anything that I can't get in the village, like nails or screws and folks will buy them for me. I live well and I don't want for anything that I need. I come down here most evenings for a pint, and I don't have to pay for it. Everyone speaks to me, but nobody comes and sits with me for long.

'Things haven't changed much around here. Only the people change. I don't know about anywhere else. I've never seen it. There's no electricity at the farm, so I don't watch TV, and I don't read any newspapers. Sometimes I go and sit on the hill and stare at the rooftops and the church spire of the next village. So near, but so far away.' He sighed again, a lonely, hopeless sigh.

'Haven't you ever tried to leave here again in all these years?'

'Yes, several times. The last time was with a young local lad who thought he was a real man of the world. He didn't quite believe my tale, you see. We set out in his car, and for all his talk, he drove dead slow as we reached the edge of the village. Lucky we did! His engine blew up and the bonnet shot open. He broke his nose and cut his face on the dashboard. I was alright, of course, as always, but he needed ten stitches.' He sighed deeply again.

'I shouldn't grumble really. It's a nice village. And things are looking up for me. I've had a couple of twinges in my knees over the past few months. Apart from the cramps when I've tried to get away, and the grief when my dear Caroline died, it's the only physical pain I've ever felt! The mental pain's often been there though, I can tell you. I'll be the first person ever to welcome arthritis like a pools win! Maybe Mother Earth hasn't got the power to keep me alive for ever, or maybe she's decided to give up and let me die at last. I hope so. I don't want to live any longer. I'll be happy to be laid at rest at last, tucked away inside the Earth that's owned me for so long.

'Oh well, tomorrow's another day as they say, and I've got a farm to run.' Dan finished his beer, wiped his mouth with the back of his hand, and stood up. He looked down at Jilly and his old eyes twinkled in his young face for a moment. Then he politely touched his hand to his forehead and walked out into the misty rain. An icy blast entered the pub before he shut the door.

Jilly picked up her untouched drink and hurried to the window, watching him walking along the road, his arms dangling beside him, his shoulders hunched against the fine, soaking rain, and the heavy burden that he had to carry through life.

She walked back to the bar and Bill the landlord eyed her with a slight smile, waiting for her reaction.

'It can't be true!' she burst out, 'It just can't be!'

'Can't it?' It was more a statement than a question.

'But 200 years old? It's impossible!'

Bill placed both hands on the bar and leaned forwards. 'It is true,' he said, 'I've owned this pub for nearly 40 years and my Dad and Grandad owned it before me, and several generations before them. I remember Dan when I was a small boy. He used to come in here every evening, and he looked just the same as he does now. He gets his pint, and insists on paying for it with half a dozen eggs, some veg or a couple of pork chops.'

'Well then, aren't you having a big celebration for his birthday? Won't he get a telegram from the Queen?'

Bill shook his head. 'Dan wouldn't like that. And the outside world doesn't know he exists. We've always protected our Dan.'

'Yes, but wouldn't it be a help to him if we told the Press? He'd make lots of money and they may be able to help him somehow.'

'Now don't you go telling anyone, Miss.' Bill was still smiling but his eyes had turned cold and threatening. 'Dan doesn't need any money. He's got nothing to spend it on. And we don't want a load of them paparazzi swarming all over our village. If they did turn up, nobody would talk to them, and we'd all just laugh and say that Dan's a good storyteller and he's been pulling your leg.'

'Well why did you let him tell me then?' Jilly wailed.

The landlord regarded her sympathetically. 'Because it does him good to talk about it sometimes. It helps to pass the time for him, and you seemed like a sensible girl.'

Jilly still wasn't sure about everything. 'But what about my writing the story then?'

'You go ahead and write your story,' Bill told her, 'But don't you use the real name of our village, or anyone here. Write it as though it's a piece of fiction, and protect our anonymity.'

So that is what I did.

Just Once More

She was late. She was always late.

She'd tried to make it on time, but she kept finding more things that she had to do before she left home, to postpone that dreadful moment when she'd know that she was helpless, under his power again.

There wasn't a parking space anywhere! A feeling of panic started to develop in her chest and her clammy hands slipped on the steering-wheel as she drove around the block for the third time.

Oh, why had she phoned him? Why? She didn't want to see him again; she was dreading it, but she couldn't bear the pain, the physical ache, if she didn't go to him.

Just once more, just one more time, then it would all be over at last.

But she had to hurry.

Half relieved, half disappointed, she spotted a winking indicator ahead of her and she eased the car into the departing van's empty space.

Grabbing her handbag, she locked the car and began to run, dodging the pedestrians who all seemed to be trying to stop her passing.

At last she reached the familiar blue door and she leaned against the wall beside it, waiting for her heartbeat to slow down.

She was too late! She must be! Oh please let him wait! But she knew that he would. He always did, with that soothing smile of his, never angry with her.

Why didn't she turn and hurry back the way she'd come, melting into the crowds on the pavement? He didn't know she was there outside the door.

But she knew that she couldn't turn back now. Things had gone too far. She had to see him. Just once more.

Slowly, she turned the door handle. It was unlocked. She closed the door behind her and gazed up the fifteen stairs. Fifteen. She always counted them.

Grasping the banister rail, she hauled herself reluctantly upwards. One, two, three, four, come on, keep going. Five, six, seven, eight, oh, she was out of breath already! Hurry, get it over with! Nine, ten, eleven, twelve, she could picture him there, at the top of the stairs to the right, waiting for her, listening to her approaching footsteps. Thirteen, unlucky for some, ha ha, fourteen, fifteen.

And there he was, smiling at her. He turned and she followed him with meek, robotic steps. He helped her out of her coat, then her legs lost all their remaining strength and she collapsed into the chair behind her.

Gripping the arms of the chair, she tried to control herself as his face came nearer, nearer to hers. Then she closed her eyes and her lips reluctantly parted.

At last he spoke. 'Ah yes, you need a small filling at the top here. I'll just give you an injection to stop the pain. And try to relax, Mrs Janner. I promise I won't hurt you. I never do, do I?'

Nelly the Pig

As soon as Janice Drayton hit 30 she started piling on the pounds.

Reg, her Dad, was starting to worry. Janice had never been a beauty and if she was beginning to decline at such a young age she'd never find a husband. She'd always loved her food, and as Reg ran a pub there was usually plenty of it about.

The trouble was that Janice was a very laid-back, easy-going lass. She'd never followed fashions or taken a lot of care of her appearance.

'Janice, Luv, he said to her one day after closing time, when they'd finally managed to evict the reluctant stragglers, 'Isn't it time you found a husband and made me a Grandad?'

His daughter giggled. 'Oh Dad, who's going to pick me? And who'd look after you if I wasn't here? Anyway, all the customers are already married.'

'Now don't you worry about me,' Reg reassured her, 'I'd be fine.' He reached in his back pocket and pulled out a wad of notes. He peeled off some £20s and handed them to her. 'Here you are. Why don't you go into town tomorrow and treat yourself to some nice clothes? And some new makeup as well. Go mad. And get your hair re-styled. It's due for a trim anyway isn't it?' he said tactfully.

But Reg would never have encouraged Janice to change her appearance if he'd known that she'd make advances to Olwen Gittins. Tight Gittins as he was known.

Every evening Olwen would sit nursing his half of bitter. He'd never bought anyone else a drink, although he never minded taking free drinks from other people.

When the newly-transformed Janice appeared, everyone made jokes and voiced their approval, while Olwen sat on his bar stool watching, with one mittened hand wrapped round his glass.

Janice smiled at him as she passed.

'Can I get you a lemonade or something?' Olwen suddenly asked her.

'Ooh, thanks!' Janice giggled shyly. Olwen was a lot older than her.

The whole bar went quiet. They all watched in amazement as Olwen produced his little worn leather purse from his jacket pocket. He opened it and counted coins into his hand until he had the right amount.

'Mind the moths don't escape, Olwen!' someone called out.

'There's no harm in being careful in life,' Olwen replied.

'Cheers,' Janice said, raising her glass of lemonade and clinking it against Olwen's bitter.

They spent the rest of the evening with their heads together, talking quietly.

Reg pretended not to notice when Janice went outside soon after Olwen left.

As she clambered into Olwen's landrover, Janice tried to ignore the smell of animals, hay, mud and other things.

Olwen couldn't believe his luck with this young female coming on to him so openly. And her Dad ran the local pub too! He reached over and grabbed hold of her.

Rearranging her clothes as she climbed out, Janice fought her disappointment. Was that it then? If so, what was all the fuss about? Oh well, perhaps it got better with a bit of practice, and being tucked up in a bed instead of in the back of a car.

She quietly opened the pub door and crept up the stairs.

Reg heard her bedroom door shut. A cold chill passed through him. He turned on his side and pulled the duvet over his shoulders.

The 'courtship,' if it could be called that, only lasted a few weeks.

'She'll do,' Olwen thought, 'And she looks fertile. I need some sons to keep the farm going.'

As he stood drying glasses, Reg wondered if he'd done the right thing, encouraging Janice to find a man. He'd asked his daughter what she saw in Olwen Gittins.

'Well, he's got nice, um, er, - blue eyes! Yes, he's got nice eyes,' she said reluctantly.

Reg sighed. At least Janice would be well-off. Olwen Gittins must be worth a fortune.

It was a simple wedding. Janice wore a blue lace dress. She had a flower behind her ear.

Olwen wore a dark blue suit. The trousers were about an inch too short and the style was very out of date.

'Nice suit, Olwen,' said one of the guests sarcastically.

'Yeah,' Olwen proudly smirked, 'It was my Dad's. We were nearly the same size, except he was shorter than me.' He looked downwards. 'It had a bit of a stain on the jacket, but I think I got it all out.'

Reg closed the pub for a few hours in the morning to go and see his only daughter marry a farmer who was just a few years younger than him. Then it was back to the pub for a buffet lunch and free drinks.

Olwen suddenly developed a thirst as he wasn't paying. He had several halves of bitter and then changed to drinking double whiskies.

'Are you sure you're okay to drive?' Reg asked his new son-in-law doubtfully as he helped Janice to climb into the landrover with her suitcase and kissed her goodbye.

'Sure, I'm fine. Besides, it's only a few miles up the road,' Olwen slurred.

Janice waved to all the customers as they drove off. Her Dad watched them until they were out of site. Then, fighting back the tears, he went in to serve drinks to the celebrating guests.

Fumbling for the key in his trousers pocket, Olwen staggered slightly.

'Aren't you going to carry me across the threshold?' Janice asked him as he opened the door, batting her eyelashes hopefully.

'You're joking! What, with my back?' Olwen retorted, 'come on, bring your case in.'

With a sigh, Janice lifted up her suitcase and walked inside her new home.

Grabbing hold of his young wife, Olwen kissed her passionately. Janice hopefully kissed him back, trying not to reach as his whisky-flavoured tongue slobbered around in her mouth. Then Olwen took hold of her wrist and rushed up the stairs, pulling her along behind him.

He pushed Janice on the bed and fell on top of her.

She just had a few seconds to see the state of the room, then she shut her eyes and tried to concentrate on sex with her new husband.

Pulling off his jacket, trousers and shoes, Olwen got under the covers. Janice was still fully-dressed.

It only took a few minutes, then Olwen rolled off her. Janice lay staring at the ceiling, a lifetime away from an orgasm.

'Well,' she thought, 'I've heard of Englishmen keeping their socks on, but never their mittens!'

With a frustrated sigh, she turned towards Olwen and started to undo his shirt buttons.

'What are you doing? Gettoff!' he protested.

Janice was surprised and hurt. 'I thought we could have a bit of a cuddle. You know, naked.' She said shyly.

He pushed her hand away. 'Are you joking? There's a North-Easterly due later tonight. And I've got to get up early to see to the cows.'

So that was the Gittins' honeymoon night.

Janice dreamt that she was in the back of Olwen's landrover, being shaken around. Then she realised that it was Olwen roughly shaking her.

'Come on, you can't stay in bed all day!' was his romantic greeting to his new wife.

'Huh? What time is it?' she asked.

'Nearly five. Now you take it easy today and just do things in the house. I'll be back at nine for my cooked breakfast.' Then Olwen pulled on a shapeless pair of corduroy trousers and a battered check jacket and she heard him going down the rickety stairs, creak, thud, creak, thud, followed by the bang of the front door.

Rolling over again, Janice tried to go back to sleep. Then she saw the colour of the pillow. 'Yuck!' she screamed, leaping out of bed. As she pulled back the covers she noticed a tiny black insect scuttling for cover. And she saw the circle of bites around her ankle.

Oh this was horrible! Janice searched in the huge musty oak drawers for clean sheets, but she couldn't find any.

She stripped off her wedding dress and went into the bathroom. Turning on the bath taps, she ran her hand under them. She waited and waited, but the water didn't get any hotter.

The airing-cupboard was along the landing. She bent down and turned on the immersion heater switch.

While the water got hot, Janice decided to unpack her case. She opened the huge oak wardrobe and stepped back in horror. It was jam-packed with old clothes. And the smell went down the back of her throat.

She took a gulp of air and lifted out as many clothes as she could manage. There were dresses dating back to the 1940s and several fur coats. She dropped them on the floor. Then she ran herself a bath and soaked in the water while she wondered what on earth she'd let herself in for.

Olwen came back at nine on the dot. Janice had prepared a fried breakfast for him with thickly buttered bread. She was a good cook and proud of it.

Turning on the tap to wash his hands, Olwen let out a squeal. 'What's this?' he asked.

'Um, water?' Janice replied. She didn't know what else to say.

'Yes, but it's HOT!'

'I know. I switched the immersion heater on for my bath. I don't know how else you heat the water.'

'Is it still on? Is it?' Olwen asked her.

'Well, yes, I suppose so.' Janice nervously bit her lip.

'Oh my God! Do you think I'm made of money?' Olwen shouted. (Well actually he never shouted. He just whined a bit louder.) Then he stormed up the stairs, followed by Janice. He threw the airing-cupboard door open and switched the heater off.

'But how am I supposed to bath?' Janice asked her husband.

'Bath? What do you want to bath for? You haven't got time for all that. You've got work to do, and you'll only get dirty again, won't you?' Then he stormed into the bedroom.

He paused and picked up one of the dresses. 'What's my Mum's clothes doing on the floor?' he asked.

Janice decided to speak up. 'There's no room in the wardrobe for my clothes. And – and your Mum's dead!'

'Well they're good clothes. We don't throw good things away. You never know when they'll come in handy. You just pick them all up and put them back. And what's happened to the bed? Are you too lazy to make it?' he asked.

Swallowing, Janice continued, 'the sheets are filthy. Where do you keep the clean ones?'

'Clean ones?' Olwen whined, 'What do you think this is, a bloody hotel?'

'But there are fleas in the bed!' Janice persisted.

'Course there are fleas in the bed!' Olwen said, 'This is a farm, with animals on it! If you want to be fussy, you can wash the sheets and put them back on again.'

He stomped downstairs to eat his breakfast. Janice followed him in time to hear the next complaint.

'What's this?' he demanded, holding up a slice of bread.

'It's called bread.' Janice tried to joke.

'You must have about half a pack of marge on here. Are you trying to bankrupt me, or kill me off with heart trouble?' Olwen scraped his knife along the bread, removing as much marge as he could.

Trying to keep calm, Janice found a duster and a tin of polish in a cupboard and she started to dust the filthy shelves, putting old ornaments and bits and pieces of rubbish on the floor. There were cotton reels, scissors, buttons, an empty tin, something mouldy and unidentifiable, and a load of other items.

Tutting, Olwen slapped down his knife and fork. 'What are you up to now? He demanded.

'I'm sorting out the mess here,' she retorted.

'Why don't you just leave things alone?' he snarled, 'They were my Mum's things.'

'Was it her dust too?' Janice snapped back.

That's when she received her first slap.

'Don't you be so lippy,' Olwen told her. Then he loudly slurped the rest of his tea and stomped out.

Janice made a stew with leftover bits from the fridge, a couple of potatoes and some tinned tomatoes.

Olwen obviously enjoyed it and it put him in a good mood.

'We need some shopping,' she said.

'Olwen nodded. 'you make a list and I'll work out the cost.'

The next day she gave him the list and he calculated how much it came to. And when she got home, he carefully checked the list and held his hand out for the change.

Every morning, rain or shine, Olwen woke her at five. Janice gave up trying to improve the house. Instead, she threw herself into the life of the farm. She watched Olwen as he worked, and asked questions, which seemed to please him. As she was lonely and missed the life of the pub, she made a fuss of all the animals. And they obviously loved her too.

She hated Olwen. They lived their life together in virtual silence, but every now and then, one of them would explode and Olwen would hit out at her.

When Janice asked to borrow the landrover to visit her Dad and Olwen refused, calling it a waste of fuel, she yelled at him, saying she was bored out of her skull.

'Well if you managed to produce some kids, you wouldn't be bored, would you?' he whined.

'Fat chance of that with you firing blanks!' she retorted.

She got the worst slapping around that she'd ever had then. She was covered in bruises in between the flea bites.

Moving painfully, Janice tipped Nelly the Pig's feed in the trough.' Here you are, Nelly,' she sighed.

'Thanks Janice,' said Nelly the Pig.

Janice froze with the bucket in her hand.

'Did you just speak?' she asked.

'Well who did you think it was? said Nelly the Pig.

'Oh thank goodness!' Janice laughed, 'I've been so lonely! I've got no-one to talk to!'

'Nor have I,' said Nelly the Pig, 'What's wrong with you today?'

'Olwen hit me.'

'Huh,' said Nelly the Pig.

A few days later, Janice stepped carefully through the muddy area next to the sty. She opened the gate and tipped Nelly the Pig's food into the trough.

'Morning, Nelly,' she said, 'You haven't seen Olwen have you? I can't find him anywhere.'

'He's having sex,' said Nelly the Pig, burying her snout in the trough.

'You WHAT? Where? Who with?' Janice wailed.

Nelly the Pig raised her snout and looked round at Janice. 'With Peggy the Postie. They've been at it for years.'

'Where are they?' shrieked Janice. Just because she hated Olwen it didn't mean that he could have sex with anyone else!

'In the barn,' said Nelly the Pig and buried her snout firmly in the trough again.

'Aaaaaaoooow!' Janice cried. She dropped the bucket and stormed off to the barn, slipping in the mud.

Peggie the Postie was just climbing into her van. She had hay sticking out of her dyed-blonde hair. She smirked at Janice.

Olwen came out of the barn, fastening the belt of his trousers. He paused, mid-buckling, when he saw Janice. 'What are you doing here?' he asked defensively, 'Haven't you got any work to do?'

Janice turned and hurried away. She had to think about this situation very carefully. Although she hated Olwen, she'd become fond of the farm. She didn't want to lose it; especially to a great lump like Peggy the Postie!

The weeks passed and the liaison regularly continued. Olwen would send Janice to work on something at the other side of the farm when Peggy the Postie was due. Janice secretly simmered with rage.

'I hate Olwen!' she confessed to Nelly the Pig early one morning.

'Kill him then,' said Nelly the Pig.

'What?' Janice gasped. Had she heard right? 'But what would I do with the body?'

'Pigs eat anything,' said Nelly the Pig.

Janice paused for a minute, thinking. 'I don't know if I could do it. Could I?' she asked herself.

'Please yourself,' said Nelly the Pig.

Olwen came in at nine for his breakfast and starting moaning about Janice's lack of economy. Then he looked up. Something about her expression wasn't quite right.

'What are you looking at me like that for?' he demanded.

'I'm just thinking what a miserable, tight git you are, Gittins,' she bravely told him.

Slowly he put down his knife and fork and advanced on her. 'What did you say?' he asked, wondering if he'd heard her correctly.

Janice backed away. 'Going deaf are you?' she taunted, 'Why don't you pick on someone your own size?'

'You what? I don't believe this. I-' then he lost his temper and threw himself at her.

After slapping her until she screamed, Olwen turned to finish his breakfast.

All that Janice could see in front of her was a red glow. She had completely lost control.

Picking up one of the late Mrs Gittins' brass ornaments, she crashed it down on Olwen's skull.

He looked up at her, then he went cross-eyed and his eyes slowly glazed over.

Janice moved his plate before his head landed in the eggs and bacon.

She went and sat down in the lounge, trying to make her breathing slow down. She kept peeping in the kitchen to make sure that he was still there. He was, with his head resting on the table.

Forcing herself to go in there again, she picked up the brass ornament and, rubbing it over with the sleeve of her jumper to hide her fingerprints, she carefully placed it back in exactly the same place, surrounded by dust.

Janice was a strong lady and Olwen was light and weedy. He had a dent in his skull, but it hadn't broken the skin, so there was no blood. She bent down and, letting Olwen's body slump on to her, she hoisted him over her shoulder and carried him to the pig-sty, feeling her way carefully so that she didn't slip in the mud.

With a bit of difficulty she managed to push him over the wall where he landed face-down in the mud.

Nelly the Pig looked up from her eating.

'There you are, Nelly, lunch.' Janice told her friend.

'I'm not hungry at the moment,' said Nelly the Pig.

'Oh come on, Nelly,' Janice encouraged her, 'You told me that pigs would eat anything. You can do it as revenge for all the people that eat pigs.'

'People eating pigs? What are you talking about?' said Nelly the Pig.

Janice thought. 'Oh come on Nelly, you must have heard of pork chops? Roast pork with apple sauce?'

'No I have not!' said Nelly the Pig, 'Eurrrgh, you've put me right off now!'

'Please eat him, Nelly, or I'll get into trouble.'

'Well that's not my problem, is it?' said Nelly the Pig.

Janice splodged through the mud and went to feed the chickens. Then she trudged back to the sty and peeped over the wall. Olwen was still where she'd left him.

'Oh please help me, Nelly!' she begged, 'Please!'

'No, sorry, I don't fancy him,' said Nelly the Pig, 'Maybe you should have ground him up with my food. I don't think I could eat a whole one.'

Thinking desperately, Janice pleaded, 'Well can't you just nibble him a bit round the edges?'

'Nibble him round the edges? What do you take me for?' said Nelly the Pig.

Feeling panic rising, Janice plodded through the mud again and went back to the house.

How was the timing? She'd fed the pigs at about seven and she'd killed Olwen at nine. When should she call the police and say that he'd disappeared? Tomorrow morning. Yes, she'd go to feed the pigs, then say that she'd found him dead in the sty.

Why hadn't she missed him all night? Because she often went to bed early and he got up early.

Perfect! He must have slipped in the mud and banged his head on the wall.

Surprisingly, Janice slept well that night. She got up at six, dressed and went to feed the pigs.

'Morning Nelly,' she called as she approached the sty. She peeped over the wall. Olwen was still lying in the mud, un-nibbled. 'Damn!' muttered Janice, 'You've really let me down, Nelly.'

'It was the pork chops that did it,' said Nelly the Pig.

Janice went back to the house and called the police. She pressed 3, then 5, then 3 again as instructed, and listened to a voice saying that all lines were busy, but her call was very important to them, so would she please wait and someone would be with her soon.

Janice wondered if hundreds of battered wives had finished off their husbands and they were all calling the police to tell them.

Finally someone spoke and she told them that she'd found her husband in the pig-sty and she thought he was dead and would they please hurry as she didn't know what to do.

She was told that they were quite busy at the moment, but the police would be with her some time that morning.

Janice made a cup of tea and sat down for a while, thinking about what had happened, and about what could happen.

She would inherit the farm! She'd throw out all the rubbish and make it a lovely home. And maybe she'd find a kind, caring husband to love her and look after her.

She pictured a gorgeous man holding her in his arms and-

What was that noise? A car? A van?

Peering out the window, Janice was horrified to see Peggy the Postie's van slipping over the ruts of the drive. Then it stopped by the barn.

Janice crept out and slid along the muddy path to the pig-sty. She wondered for a split second if Nelly the Pig would enjoy a big, juicy postwoman.

No, probably not.

She could hear Peggy the Postie shouting in a whisper. (Why did people do that?)

'Olwen! Olwen! Are you there?' Then she came out of the barn and started snooping around.

Janice reached the sty at the same time as Peggy the Postie peered over the wall.

'Aoooooowwww, Olwen!' she wailed.

Jumping back and crouching behind the wall, Janice thought desperately. Hopefully Peggy the Postie would go in the sty and move Olwen about a bit, which would destroy some of the evidence with a bit of luck.

Unfortunately, Janice slipped in the mud and couldn't keep her balance. She fell backwards and slithered down the slope, gaining speed and bumping into Peggy the Postie.

It's unsure who started it first. It was probably a combination of anger and lack of balance. Suddenly both women were rolling in the mud, punching and head-butting each other.

Luckily at that moment a spare police car that was in the area arrived, as it would almost definitely have been a fight to the death.

'Pete, stop those women fighting,' said Big Al the senior PC, who then looked over the pig-sty wall and noticed the body lying face-down.

'Oh no,' he groaned, 'I should be off this afternoon! I was going to watch the match with my mates.'

The last thing that Pete the PC wanted to do was to separate the women as he'd just had his uniform cleaned. He hesitated.

'Arrest those women!' Big Al ordered, pointing at them both, not knowing what else to do.

As he tried to grab hold of a mud-encrusted arm, Pete slipped in the mud and sat down. He tried to stand up, fell backwards again, and thought, 'Oh what the Hell!'

The three of them wrestled around in the mud for a while. The two women slipped out of his grasp several times, but he finally got Janice in an arm-lock and, leaning on her to keep his balance, led her towards the police-car.

Fighting against being dragged backwards, Janice shook her fist at the sty and screamed, 'You rotten pig!' ensuring a more intense autopsy for her husband than he would have got and thus, as they say, sealing her own fate.

Olwen's body was removed for tests. A temporary farm manager was brought in and things returned to normal. The sty was nice and roomy again.

The piglets were enjoying themselves in the extra space, squealing happily, pushing each other and rolling in the mud.

Their mother looked up from the trough and stared in horror.

'You children stop it at once! Look at the state of you!' said Nelly the Pig, 'You're disgusting! You should be ashamed of yourselves! You're behaving like people!'

New Start
Liberty Village

'Will you bloody kids shut up!'

'Leave them alone Bill, it's not their fault that they're stuck indoors!'

'I know. Sorry Suze. But I can't do telephone sales with that lot howling and shrieking in the background. If I could have predicted having to struggle financially so much, I'd never have had four of them!'

'Well we didn't expect to finally have twins!' Suze laughed.

Bill pointed to his laptop. 'Come here, Suze. I've been doing some research.' Suze walked over and stood beside him. He put his arm round her waist and noticed that she briefly started to pull away, then she stood still. 'I've contacted some estate agents, and you'd never believe it but this pile of crap is a highly sought-after London postal address. It's worth nearly a million. Everyone thought my parents were mad when they bought their Council flat in this stinking slum where a lot of the tenants don't know the difference between a lift and a loo!'

'Well we are on the top floor,' Suze said, digesting the information, 'If you look over the eyesores, there's a beautiful view in the distance of the City and the Thames.'

'And I found this.' Bill tapped the laptop screen with the back of his hand.

Suze leaned over his shoulder and read; Recent Vacancy for Family in Liberty Village. We're completely Self-Sufficient. Free furnished Home, Food and Clothing, Friendly Residents, plenty of Activities, all in exchange for Work Input and a small Donation!

'Sounds interesting,' Suze commented cautiously, then she winced as shouts and thumps resonated through the wall.

***

'Welcome to Liberty Village. My name is Lee. Follow me up the drive, but don't run me over, will you?'

Everyone laughed as Bill drove slowly behind the big man, who was walking quickly for someone of his size.

There were vegetables growing on both sides of the drive and the people working there looked up and waved as they passed.

'Mum, they've all got the same clothes on,' Lucy whispered.

'Shh, perhaps it's their gardening clothes,' Suze replied to her daughter.

Lee stopped outside a block of buildings. 'Here we are, Home Sweet Home,' he said, leaning in Bill's window.

Suze felt a pang of disappointment. Another poky flat. 'Which floor are we on?' she asked.

Throwing back his head, Lee laughed. 'Every floor! You've got four children, haven't you? So that's five bedrooms. It's a four-storey house! Come on, out you get. Then I'll take you to meet Colan. You can unpack and settle in at your leisure.'

They carried in a few suitcases, and the children started arguing about who was going to have which bedroom.

'I'll decide!' Bill shouted, 'Luke and Lucy on the 1st floor, William and Celia on the 2nd floor, and we'll be on the top floor. Now come on, we've got to meet the Head Honcho.'

Lee was leaning against Bill's car, smoking a herbal-smelling cigarette. He stamped on it and smiled. 'Come on, let's go and I'll introduce you to Colan. He's dying to meet you. Why don't you kids go off and explore?'

Suze looked doubtful and Lee placed his arm round her waist. 'Don't you worry, they're perfectly safe here.'

The 12-year-old twins Luke and Lucy ran off, followed more sedately by William, aged 14. Celia stayed with her parents, curious about meeting Colan.

'Here we are,' Lee stated, stopping outside a large Romanesque villa. A man stood by the front door.

'Hi Terence, this is our new Family,' Lee said.

Terence smiled and opened the door. 'Welcome to Liberty Village. Go right in. Colan's expecting you.'

'This way,' said Lee, chuckling as they stared open-mouthed at the huge hallway with a marble floor and curved marble staircase. They followed him through a carved door on the right and Lee closed the door behind them.

The room was huge, and expensively but tastefully furnished.

Colan sat on a gold-gilded chaise. 'Welcome!' he called, gesturing with his hand, 'Come and sit down!'

They perched nervously on three matching sofas. Lee stood by the door.

A woman came in, carrying a tray. She was dressed like the women in the fields, in a long coloured dress.

'Coffee?' Colan asked, 'And do make yourselves comfortable. I don't bite, you know!' He poured out the coffee and handed the cups round.

Bill tried not to stare at Colan. He was well over 6ft with long, slim legs, and wearing the same outfit as Lee and Terence; black wool trousers, a loose white cotton peasant-style shirt and leather sandals. He had black hair cut in a pageboy style, and the most piercing emerald green eyes, slanted slightly like a cat's.

'You're going to love it here, and I'm sure you'll mix in well with our Villagers,' Colan smiled, winking at Celia, who lowered her head and blushed. 'And how old are you, Suze, if you don't mind my asking a lady's age,' he continued.

'I'm 38,' Suze replied.

'Great!' Colan told her, 'So you've still got plenty of time to have a couple more children!'

'Eeouw,'said Celia, embarrassed.

'Ooh I don't know about that,' Suze giggled. Expecting her to protest, Bill stared at her and was surprised to see her nibbling on the side of her thumb and cocking her head in a flirting pose. He thought she looked ridiculous.

'And what about you, Celia. Tell me about yourself,' Colan said, leaning forwards.

Celia was blushing. 'Well there's not much to tell. I'm 16 and I was training as a hairdresser-'

'A hairdresser? That will be very useful!' Colan smiled, encouragingly. 'You'll be able to carry on with your training here – but only if you want to, of course!'

Back outside, Luke and Lucy ran up to them.

'We love it here!' gasped Lucy.

'Yeah, it's really cool,' added Luke. He was dressed in the same clothes as all the men. Lucy wore a long pink dress.

Bill pointed to them. 'So what happened to the designer gear that you've always insisted on having?' he asked.

Luke looked a bit embarrassed. 'Well there are so many cool things to do here, like a huge army-style assault course, and loads of places to explore and climb trees. And if anything gets torn or damaged, I won't get yelled at. I just go and pick another outfit. They've got hundreds.' He glared at Suze.

'Isn't my dress BEAUTIFUL! Lucy gushed, twirling round. 'They've got them in all different colours, with pretty petticoats. Come on Luke, let's go and find the others. Bye!' And they both ran off.

'Hey, have you seen William?' Suze called after them.

Luke turned his head. 'Yeah, he's with the other kids, in the woods or somewhere. Bye!'

Lee was waiting. 'Come on Bill, let's go and see what kinds of jobs you fancy,' he said. 'Why don't you wander round or do some unpacking, Suze?'

They passed some workers outside a greenhouse. One of them waved and blew a kiss.

'She fancies you,' Lee casually remarked.

Bill snorted. 'No way! Who is she?'

'Gloria. My wife. So what kind of work did you do before Liberty Village, Bill?'

'Sales mainly. Nothing manual. Can I ask you some questions?'

'Sure. Ask what you want.' Lee lit a herbal cigarette and inhaled deeply.

Wondering how to put it, Bill said, 'I haven't seen many men around.'

Lee lowered his head. 'No. It's a dangerous world out there. The Rat Race wears people down and it's often too late when they come here. It's worse for the men. They have strokes and heart attacks; even some of the younger ones. We have an excellent medical centre here, but even they can't save anyone who's too far gone.'

'Oh.' Bill digested the information. 'Well I think I'm still healthy! So what happened to the family whose place we've taken?'

There was a split second of hesitation before Lee spoke. 'Their marriage was on the rocks when they came here, and everyone got sick of their constant fighting and bickering. They weren't social people. So they had to leave. Aah, here's the carpentry workshop. Let's see if you want to do any work here. If not, there's plenty of other jobs to choose from.' He threw his cigarette end down and led the way in.

After a leisurely exploration, Bill went to meet Suze in the restaurant, which had rows of wooden tables and benches. A glorious buffet was laid out round the sides and he helped himself to a plateful of steak and chips with mixed veg, then he sat down as Suze came in. She loaded up a plate with pasta and sat down opposite him. She was wearing a long yellow dress in the same style as all the other women.

'So what have you been doing all afternoon, as if I couldn't guess!' Bill remarked sarcastically, nodding at her dress.

Suze looked guilty for a split second, then she smiled. 'Oh just this and that. Oh and Colan asked to see me again.'

'What for?' Bill stared at her and she blushed. She was doing that annoying thumb chewing again.

Celia bounced in, dressed in a matching lilac dress. 'Guess what?' she gushed, 'Colan said I'm the prettiest girl in the village and he wants to see me later!

Bill caught Suze's expression. She was glaring at her daughter and, yes, it was jealousy and almost hatred.

Something wasn't right. Bill thumped the table with his fist. 'You're not going on your own!' he snapped.

Celia jumped up. 'Why not? I can do what I like now, and you can't stop me!' She stormed out, petticoats flying.

A hand landed on Bill's shoulder. It was Lee. 'Colan wants to see you,' he ordered.

'Now? But I've just got my dinner,' Bill protested.

'There's always plenty of food and he wants to see you now. Something about you not being quite honest about your bank account.'

Bill glanced at Suze. Was she smirking? He stood up and noticed the young Village children who were all sitting together on the next table. They'd all gone quiet after he'd thumped the table and ten pairs of eyes stared straight at him.

Ten pairs of green eyes.

Nuclear Power

Rodney surveyed the remains of his neighbourhood. One day of nuclear insanity had reduced everything to a smouldering ruin – except for his house which stood there like a tooth in a tramp's head.

'I'm all alone in the world!' Rodney wailed, 'What am I going to do for clean socks?'

But what was that? Another survivor! His heart rose, then sank again as the blackened form staggered nearer. Of all the people in all the world! It had to be Lester Bradley, his neighbour! Mr Perfect Smoothy-guts! Well, look at him now. Judith wouldn't bat her eyelashes at him if she could see the state of him!

Judith! What had happened to his wife! Despite the warnings she'd gone shopping. 'Must get a few extras in, darling,' she'd insisted, 'What WILL we do if anything happens to Harrods?'

Oh well, at least she'd have died happy, clutching a credit card to her implants!

'Oh Rodney! Rodney, thank the Lord!' Lester sobbed, collapsing in a heap at Rodney's feet, 'I'm not the only one – and your house! It's still standing! Oh please, get me some water will you? My throat's killing me!'

Rodney looked down at his neighbour's bald patch and a feeling of power surged through him. Lester, Mr Popular Super-Cool, grovelling at his feet! He'd never thought he'd live to see the day!

I can be anything I like now, Rodney realised suddenly, King, Prime Minister, - even Chairman of the Rotary Club! Oh yes, I was good enough to think up all their fund-raising ideas, to organise their functions and to run around doing all the little jobs that nobody else wanted to do, but I was never popular enough to be elected as Chairman, was I?

The reigning Rotary Club Chairman clutched Rodney round the knees now, crying, 'Oh please, just a glass of water! Just lend it to me! I'll do anything you want! Anything!'

Rodney's top lip curled in a poor imitation of the late Sir Cliff Richard. 'No, I WON'T lend you any of my precious water,' he sneered, trying to shake himself free from Lester's grip. 'I'm not lending you anything!'

Lester stared up at him, a horrified expression on his blackened face. 'Why not, for the love of God?' he whimpered, muddy tears running down his cheeks.

'Becaaaause…' Rodney dragged out the words, wobbling his head, 'Becaaaause… you never returned my lawnmower!'

The Antman Cometh

Wheeling herself to the front window, Edith pushed on the brake of her wheelchair and settled down for her nightly vigil.

Dick wouldn't be back for several hours. She wondered why he bothered to come home at all. He left work and went straight to the pub until he was thrown out. And as often as not, he went off with some tart after that. Oh, he denied it, but Edith could smell the perfume and other things on him. Her legs were useless, but there was nothing wrong with her sense of smell!

She turned her nose up, aware of her own stink. When had Dick condescended to help her in and out of the bath? Weeks ago. Oh, why did she have to rely on him? She knew that he hated her. He only stayed with her because he felt sorry for her. And it was feelings mutual. If only she could walk again. Things would be a lot different then!

Watching all the people in the street ten stories below, Edith envied them their freedom. Ant people, she called them, all scurrying to and fro, or buzzing along in their little cars. They all did everything at the double. Nobody ever walked slowly at night. Fear was in the air; the primitive fear of darkness.

Edith could see clearly up and down the street through her huge picture window. It was the only decently-designed thing in her lousy Council flat.

Gradually the activity died down until the streets were nearly empty, except for the odd echoing animal howl of some bored, unemployed lout.

Why didn't the police ever turn up when they were needed? Why didn't the law clamp down on the thugs and vandals? Nobody cared about anything any more. They didn't even seem to care about themselves.

Suddenly, for a few long, drawn-out seconds, there was silence everywhere. They say it happens when an angel flies over, don't they? But, as Edith stared at the road below, it wasn't an angel she saw; it was a devil.

Stepping out of his parked car, he grabbed a young woman who was walking along on her own.

Horrified, Edith saw his knife glitter in the lamplight. Then he slid it across the struggling girl's neck and pushed her into the back of his car.

Numb with fear, Edith observed it like watching a film on the TV. And then, while he opened the driver's door, the man stared directly up at Edith as though he'd known all the time that she was watching him. His eyes glowed red in the artificial light, and he grinned, showing all his teeth. Then he leaped into his car and drove away.

When he'd gone, the street seemed to spring into life again. Cars and pedestrians appeared as the pubs spewed out their unwanted customers. Shouts and laughter filled the damp night air. The sights of a few brief seconds ago seemed like a dream – a nightmare.

Edith slammed the brake off and wheeled herself over to the phone. With a shaking hand she picked up the receiver and pressed the numbers of the local police. She knew them by heart.

'Police?' said a bored voice. He made it sound like a question.

'Hello,' Edith stammered, 'It's Mrs Parks of-'

'Oh hello, Mrs Parks.' The voice sounded even more bored. 'Yes, we know your address. Long time no hear. What is it this time – neighbours' music? Laughing kids?'

'No, it's not that.' She'd report him for his rudeness later, when she had more time. 'It – I've just witnessed a murder.'

'Oh, a murder! That's a new one!' He was obviously addressing an audience.

'Yes. Down in the road. Just now. You've got to hurry. The evidence'll be all walked over!'

There was an audible sigh down the phone. 'Alright, I'll send a couple of officers over to see you.' And the phone went dead.

Within a few minutes there was a hammering on the door.

Edith wheeled herself across the room and then she hesitated. They'd arrived quickly, hadn't they? The police usually took ages to come when she called them.

She called out, 'who is it?'

'Police, Mrs Parks.'

Sliding the chain on, Edith peered through the crack. Two policemen stood outside. She'd seen one of them before. Relieved, Edith pushed the door shut, undid the chain and opened the door.

'So what's this about a murder?' asked the policeman who she knew.

'I saw it. Just now. Over here.' Edith wheeled herself to the window and pointed. She told the police what she'd seen.

'And what did the – murderer look like? What was he wearing?' asked the same policeman. It was obviously his turn to do the talking.

'He was all in black. A black jacket; leather or something, black trousers and shoes, and a black balaclava. He looked like a giant ant. But his eyes.' Edith shuddered. 'I'll never forget his eyes. They were sort of red. And evil.'

Both police looked out of the window and then made eye-contact with each other.

'Are you telling us that you could see the colour of his eyes from up here?' asked the same policeman.

Edith nodded. 'I don't know how, but I could see them clearly. They were red. He stared right up at me, as though he knew I was watching him.'

The policemen sighed. Policemen do a lot of sighing, Edith thought to herself.

'Mrs Parks, are you sure you didn't nod off for a moment and dream all this?' asked Chatty Policeman.

She shook her head violently. 'No. No, I didn't, honestly. You've got to believe me! I saw it all! Why don't you check? There must have been a lot of blood. Go and look!'

The police looked at each other again. 'I'll go and check,' the silent one said. He went out, talking into his radio.

The remaining man spoke to Edith quietly but firmly. 'Mrs Parks, if you're making this up, I'm going to be very cross with you! In fact, I'll probably book you for wasting valuable police time. Do you understand?'

Edith nodded emphatically. 'I'm not wasting your time. You'll see!'

His radio crackled. He listened, then he spoke into it. 'Okay, I'll be right down.' He stared at Edith. 'There's no sign of any blood, Mrs Parks.'

Grabbing hold of his wrist, Edith clung on tightly with both hands. 'There is! There must be! He couldn't have looked properly! You'll see, when the girl's reported missing, and when you find her body! You'll see!'

Gently pulling his arm free, the policeman said, 'Very well, Mrs Parks, I'll make a few inquiries. The man shouldn't be too hard to spot, should he, with red eyes and a black balaclava!' And he left.

Dick came in soon after, carrying a couple of carrier-bags. 'Have you been calling the police again?' he asked, 'I saw their car leaving.'

'Oh Dick, it was awful!' his wife moaned, trying to explain what she'd seen, while he went into the kitchen and put the shopping away.

Dick said nothing. He just shook his head.

***

Edith felt a lot better. Dick had stayed in with her last night, and he'd even helped her to have a bath and wash her hair.

He'd promised to come straight home from work tonight. She'd made him a nice cottage pie and she wasn't going to moan about anything.

She wheeled herself over to her favourite position in front of the window. She could almost believe that she had nodded off for a while and dreamt it all. Almost.

And then she saw him. The Antman, she called him. He was leaning against the lamp-post, staring up at her. Just staring.

With a gasp, Edith ducked her head down. Too late. He'd obviously spotted her.

She peeped over the window-sill. He'd gone. He'd disappeared into thin air! Edith could see clearly up and down the street. He wasn't there!

Wheeling herself over to the phone, she called the police. 'Hello?' she stammered, 'It's Mrs Parks. He's been here again. The man; the murderer. He stood across the road and stared up at me. Honest! It's true! I'm not making it up! I'm not! Right, thank you. No, he's gone now, but he must be around here somewhere!'

She hung up. The police had promised to check the street, but what was the use? She knew that they wouldn't find the Antman. And she knew that they didn't believe her.

What was that? The lift! Oh no, it couldn't be HIM, could it? She wheeled herself over to the door and placed her ear against it. Someone was coming; walking towards the door!

The footsteps stopped. A key rattled in the lock and the door opened.

'Oh Dick, it's you! Oh, thank God!' she cried.

'Of course it's me,' her husband replied, 'Who did you think it was? I don't usually get welcomes like this!'

Edith pointed to the window. 'The murderer. He was outside, just now. If you'd come home a bit earlier you'd have seen him!'

Dick looked at her, and she could tell by his face that he didn't completely believe her. 'It's not one of your tricks to get me to come home earlier, is it?' he asked.

She shook her head. 'No, you must believe me. It's not! You'll see, when they find the body.' She paused, then she decided to let the subject drop. 'Sit down and I'll get you a nice cup of tea. I've made your favourite; cottage pie.'

***

The weeks went by. Dick started staying out late again, and Edith resumed her nightly position in front of the window. She phoned the police a few times to ask if they'd made any progress, but of course they hadn't. They'd probably given up trying. She wasn't surprised. When she saw the lamp-post across the road it all seemed like a realistic dream, and her fear had faded.

Then it all happened again. The Antman parked beside the light, grabbed a passing woman, cut her throat and threw her into his car. This time he looked up and waved at Edith before he drove off.

With a scream she wheeled herself across to the phone and called the police. Her hands were shaking so much that she could hardly punch in the numbers.

'He's done it again!' she cried when the phone was answered, 'the Antman! He's just killed someone else! For Gods's sake come! You must!'

***

Once again the police had arrived, interviewed her, checked the street, found nothing and gone.

Dick didn't bother staying in this time, and he didn't bother to hide his disbelief and disgust. He thought that Edith was making up the whole thing to keep him at home with her.

Edith still sat in front of the window at night, unable to stay away. She wondered if she was going mad. Perhaps her medication was making her hallucinate. Maybe she had a brain disease and everyone was right; she hadn't seen anything after all. But she had. She had, she had, she had!

And there he was again; leaning against the lamp-post, staring up at her. The Antman.

A masochistic sense of relief filled Edith's body. He was real. He was! She could see him clearly. And he could see her!

Suddenly he levered himself away from the light and started running across the road, staring up at Edith all the time. He was coming for her!

She hurried to the phone, picked up the receiver, dropped it, and picked it up again. She called the police. There was no reply; just a strange humming sound. The phone was dead! Had Dick forgotten to pay the bill?

With a gasp, Edith opened the door and wheeled herself over to the lift. She pressed the button. Nothing! The lift was out of order again! It was usually out of order at least once a week. Bloody vandals!

Then she heard it; bam bam bam! The Antman was running up the stairs! Bam bam bam, his footsteps echoed up to her. He must get tired soon! Nobody could run all the way up those stairs!

Feeling a rising panic, Edith rode across to her neighbour's door and hammered with her fists. 'Help!' she called, 'Let me in!' She heard their TV, and then it went quiet. They'd turned it off!

There were two more doors on the landing. Edith hammered on both of them, shouting for help. But nobody came out.

Why, oh why had she complained to the police so often about them all? She knew that they all hated her, but surely they wouldn't let her die, would they? And the footsteps were coming nearer, bam bam bam!

'Somebody please help me!' she screamed. But nobody answered.

Edith wheeled herself back into her flat. She slammed and locked her door and put the chain on. She tried the phone again. It was still dead.

What could she do? Could she write a note and throw it out of the window with a weight on it? No, no time.

And the footsteps came nearer, nearer. They were quieter now, coming along the landing, slower and slower. And they stopped, right outside her door.

There was the sound of heavy breathing, and a throaty laugh. He'd come for her! She was doomed!

'At least everyone will believe me now. In fact, I'll be quite famous!' Edith thought with a sense of triumph as the Antman burst through the door.

The Chef's Revenge

Apprehensively, Gina pushed open the staff door of the Wardle Manor Golf Club. It was her first day as a waitress.

She stood in the kitchen area, unsure of where to go.

'What do YOU want?' the Chef snapped, brandishing a carving-knife at her.

'Excuse me,' she asked nervously, 'Which way's the restaurant?'

The chef exploded. 'Do you think I've got nothing better to do than to stand around here giving epping instructions all day?' he screamed, 'I'm up to my epping eyes in work! Fat lot of epping use you're going to be if you can't even find your epping way round the epping place!'

Donald the restaurant manager came out of a nearby door. 'Hi Gina,' he said, 'Right, follow me. This place is like a maze. It's through here and up the stairs.'

'You ought to get yourself some epping staff with epping brains!' the Chef yelled after them, 'And you can tell that epping Colonel Fortescue that if he complains about my food again today, I'll ram it down his epping throat!'

'Nice man,' Gina commented.

Donald nodded. 'Yeah, right. Great Chef too. His food's tasteless, he can't get his quantities right, and he's a right bad-tempered pig.'

'Well why do they keep him on?'

'Because the Club Manager's terrified of him!' Donald pushed a door open. 'Right. This is Gina,' he announced to the group that was hovering around, unsure of what to do. 'This is Elly, Cara, Annie and Colin.'

They all said hello, except Cara, who was gazing at Donald as though he was a pop star.

'Donald, we're ten bread rolls short!' Annie called across the restaurant.

'Um, right. Well phone the Chef and tell him,' Donald ordered.

Annie looked as though she was going to the dentist's as she walked into the servery. She slowly picked up the phone and said, 'This is the restaurant here. We're ten rolls short.' She listened, then a slow flush spread up her neck. Bursting into tears, she grabbed her handbag and ran out.

'Annie!' Where are you going?' Donald called after her.

'Home!' she sobbed.

'Right,' said Donald, following the crying waitress, 'I'll sort this out.'

'They're coming in!' Elly called, 'Tell the kitchen to send the soup up.'

Gina swallowed. 'Oh, um, okay.' She picked up the phone, breathed in and said, 'The members are here. Can we have the soup please?' and hung up.

Donald reappeared. His breath smelt of whisky.

When the soup came up in the dumb waiter, he ladled it into bowls and the staff carried them into the restaurant.

Suddenly, one of the members leaped to his feet and waved his arm in the air, shouting, '-And he hit the first birdie of the day!'

Three bowls of hot soup shot over Elly. Screaming, she dropped the empty bowls on the floor and ran out of the restaurant, clutching her face and left bust.

Donald rushed after her and came back a few minutes later. 'Right,' he said, 'Elly's gone to hospital. We're down to five of us, so we'll all have to work harder. Ah, right, here's the main course.' He began to take the food out of the lift.

Cara poked the cauliflower with her finger. 'Donald,' she cooed, gazing into his eyes, 'This cauliflower's stone cold.'

The Clubhouse Manager burst through the door. 'What's going on?' he demanded, 'We've been waiting for ages!'

Donald patted the cauliflower. 'The cauliflower's cold,' he said.

'Okay, I'll deal with this,' the Clubhouse Manager said, swallowing nervously. He picked up the dish and went off to the kitchen.

He reappeared surprisingly quickly, wearing sprigs of cauliflower on his head and shoulders. 'Um, cauliflower's off,' he muttered and left the room.

Gina carried out three plates of beef goulash. One of the members beckoned to her. 'I'm a vegetarian,' he told her, 'Could I have something else?'

'And could I have another bread roll, darling?' his neighbour asked.

Plucking up her courage, Gina went in the servery and picked up the phone. 'Have you got anything for a vegetarian?' she asked the Chef.

'Yeah, an epping bunch of fives!' he yelled.

Gina swallowed and then persisted, 'Could you send something up for a vegetarian, please?'

'No I epping couldn't!' the Chef bawled, 'Do they think I keep a stack of spare epping meals down here? He couldn't think to epping tell me in advance, could he? Epping prats!'

'And someone wants another bread roll.'

'Oh for Chrissakes! What do they think this is – an epping bakery?' And the phone went dead.

Gina shrugged, not knowing if the Chef was going to sort everything out or ignore it.

'Right,' said Donald, 'I'll deal with this.' And he went out.

Hesitantly, Gina walked into the restaurant and smiled at everyone, wondering what to do next.

One of the members waved her over. 'Excuse me, dear,' he said, 'Could you tell the Chef that the goulash is a bit watery, and there's not much meat in it.'

While he spoke, his hand slid round her waist and down to her bottom. She backed away out of his reach.

'Right, I'll tell him,' she muttered, feeling the colour drain out of her face.

With a sigh, she picked up the phone. Her hand was shaking. 'One of the members asked me to tell you that the goulash is a bit watery and-'

Gina had never met a werewolf. But she was sure that if she ever did, it would sound just like the Chef.

Donald came back in time to hear the unearthly howls coming out of the phone. His eyes were a bit glazed. 'Right,' he said, breathing whisky fumes towards Gina, 'Arrange the cheese biscuits on plates, will you?'

She'd just finished arranging them when Cara dashed in, laden with dirty plates. She knocked three of the cheese plates on the floor with her elbow and then dropped all the cutlery off the top of the dirty plates.

'Right,' slurred Donald, 'Pick the biscuits up and rearrange them, will you?'

'I'll help you,' Colin told her, picking up the biscuits and rubbing the dirt off them.

After the apple crumble was finally served, followed by the cheese and biscuits and coffee, Donald said, 'Right, the members are having their prize-giving now, so I'm just going out for a quick fag.'

'I'll come with you, Donald!' Cara called, trotting along behind him.

One of the members was speaking into the microphone, trying to ignore the squeaks and whistles. Suddenly he broke off in mid-sentence. A murmur spread around the room. The staff peeped out of the door in time to see him drop the mike, clutch his stomach and dash out of the room, gradually followed by most of the members.

'Right, wha'sapp'ning?' Donald stammered, weaving back into the servery and leaning against the wall.

Colin shrugged. 'No idea.'

The Clubhouse Manager burst in. 'What's going on?' he asked, 'All the members are running into the toilet!'

Gina gasped. 'It must be the dirty biscuits! We've poisoned them!'

The Chef crashed through the door and everyone backed away. His hair was a mess and his eyes looked wild. He resembled a werewolf now, instead of just sounding like one. 'Ha!' he howled, 'That'll teach them! I put laxatives in the epping crumble!'

'Now really,' sighed the Clubhouse Manager, 'I think we'd better have a few words about this!'

'You can have two words!' the Chef screamed, 'And the second one's –off!'

Donald slid down the wall, giggling. Cara crouched next to him, putting her hand on his shoulder.

'-And you can stick your epping job where the sun don't shine!' bawled the Chef, stepping over Donald and storming out.

'I say!' called the Clubhouse Manager, 'Does that mean you won't be in tomorrow?'

The werewolf howl drifted back into the servery.

Gina snatched up her handbag. 'And I won't be in tomorrow either,' she announced as she left, 'This place is a madhouse!'

Donald shrieked with laughter, tears pouring down his face. The Clubhouse Manager went off to find someone to sort everything out for him.

Driving past the golf course, Gina was sure that it was the Chef who she could see in the distance, running and leaping across the grass with his arms outstretched and flapping up and down like a bird. Only he wasn't wearing any clothes.

The Last Trick

They were certainly a wonderful audience tonight! None of his tricks were original, but The Great Marvello performed them with dignity and an original style, and he was always popular. But tonight's audience were really enjoying themselves.

The Great Marvello glanced at Maisy, his wife and partner for fifteen years. She'd captured the atmosphere too, because her eyes were shining and her cheeks were flushed. She'd kept her slim, boyish figure, so she still looked attractive in her skimpy costume, and she knew it! She knew how to play to the audience too. She caught his eye and he winked at her. She smiled back. Yes, he was a lucky man. He loved his work, and he had the perfect wife and partner. And in a fortnight's time they were leaving on a three months' world cruise, with all expenses paid – the best booking they'd ever had. Oh yes, he was a lucky man alright!

It was their Grand Finale. Maisy dragged two 'volunteers' out of the audience; two strong men to help her handcuff The Great Marvello and wrap him in chains. The two men tugged and pulled at the chains and padlocks to make sure they were genuine, then they lifted the magician into a sack, which they tied and padlocked at the top, picked him up between them and lowered him into a tank filled with water. Then a tent-like cover dropped down, hiding the tank from the audience's view.

It was an old, well-known trick and Maisy was always surprised at the growing concern on the faces that she could vaguely see in the front rows. A murmuring gradually increased as the seconds ticked past, and the music roared to a crescendo, playing on the atmosphere.

She posed in front of the covered tank, smiling reassuringly at the audience, but gradually beginning to wear her 'worried' face as time went by.

The Great Marvello relaxed in the warm water. This was one of his favourite tricks. He'd practically doubled the length of time that he could hold his breath since he'd starting performing the trick, nearly fifteen years ago. He was aiming to appear in the Guinness Book of Records for the longest time spent under water before escaping, so he always held on until the last possible second before he started to free himself.

Oh well, time to go…

***

Maisy watched through her black veil as The Great Marvello's coffin was lowered into the grave. He won't be escaping from there, she thought cynically, turning to leave, while a few friends gently patted her on the shoulder, asking her if she was alright.

She recalled the scene, just a week ago, when everyone had finally realised that something had gone wrong. The manager had rushed onto the stage, followed by a group of assistants. They'd wrenched off the huge cover and hauled The Great Marvello's body out of the water, tearing at the sack to release him. Maisy had fallen on top of his wet, lifeless body, screaming hysterically and tugging at the handcuffs and chains.

'Marv, speak to me! You can't be dead!' she'd sobbed, 'Not after fifteen years!'

Fifteen miserable years she'd put up with him, bossing her about, humiliating her, and carrying on with every female he could lay his hands on.

In all the confusion, nobody had seen her remove the tiny piece of metal that she'd used to jam the release catch on the handcuffs.

She'd decided that she was still going on the world cruise, but as a passenger, not a performer, thanks to the large insurance settlement.

And she never needed to work again. The Great Marvello and Maisy had both performed their last trick.

Village People

'Oh Shawn, isn't this heaven?'

'Yeah. Aren't you glad I talked you out of booking a package holiday?'

Geena nodded, leaning her back against the car's warm metal and staring at the panoramic view stretching for miles in every direction.

Weirdly twisted olive trees clung to the side of the terraced mountains; tiny villages perched precariously above them where the air was much cooler than a few miles lower down in tourist land, and in the distance the sea shimmered invitingly in the sunlight.

It had been a long drive through France, but it had been worth it. They were free to point the car in any direction they fancied.

'I'm gasping for a drink,' Shawn said, putting his arm round her, 'Pick a village.'

'Um, that one over there.' Geena pointed to the top of the next mountain.

'Okay, vamonos!'

Half an hour later they parked in the village square, in the shade of the huge ornate church. Half a dozen bars were clustered round the square.

'Which one do you fancy?' Shawn asked.

Geena shrugged. 'They all look the same. Let's go in the nearest.'

Loud voices greeted them as they opened the door. Then silence fell and everyone turned and stared at them; everyone except two men who were bent over a game of dominoes.

'I thought the natives were meant to be friendly,' Shawn muttered, smiling and nodding around him. Nobody smiled back.

Geena hesitated. 'Shall we go?' But Shawn took hold of her elbow and led her to the bar.

'No, I'm dying for a beer and I bet their prices are cheap, even if their hospitality's not too hot. Dos cervezas por favor,' he said to the unsmiling barman, who opened two bottles and placed them on the counter, then he reached under the counter for the glasses and placed them beside the beers, and as he did he leaned forward and stared into Shawn and Geena's faces.

Geena felt shivers travel down the back of her neck.

She picked up her beer and turned to find a table. And she gasped. The bar had been full when they'd come in; now it was empty except for the two dominoes players. But she hadn't heard anyone shout goodbye or open the door.

'Where's everyone disappeared to?' Shawn asked loudly in a mock-jolly voice.

'Do you think they all left because we came in?' Geena realised she was whispering.

Shawn shook his head. 'It's only 10.30. They've probably all had their elevenses and gone back to work.'

'I suppose so,' Geena agreed, but she perched nervously on the edge of her chair and kept glancing in every direction as she drank her beer.

The barman stared at them while they talked. Then he turned and called into the kitchen behind him. A woman who was obviously his wife came out and stood beside him. She was dressed completely in black and permanently-etched frown lines creased her forehead. With her arms folded she silently studied Shawn and Geena.

Geena was about to leave when a beautiful girl aged about seven skipped out from the doorway behind the bar. She was wearing a white flounced dress and her long dark hair hung in ringlets with a white bow at the back. She was singing but she stopped beside Geena and Shawn and silently glared at them.

'Oh isn't she lovely?' Geena called to the woman. She reached out a hand to the girl, saying, 'Hola!'

The girl stared with huge green eyes, and then her teeth bared in an animal-like snarl. She snapped at Geena's hand, but Geena withdrew it just in time as the woman in black shouted at the girl who ran back behind the bar.

'My God, talk about inbreeding!' Shawn muttered, finishing his beer.

Geena was shaking. 'Let's get out of here NOW!' she pleaded.

They rushed to the door, trying to act casual, turning to nod a goodbye to the family.

A bent old lady dressed in black was shuffling towards them with a hostile expression on her wrinkled brown face. Shawn and Geena both grabbed at the door handle at the same time and rushed out, shutting the door behind them.

Shawn unlocked the car and started the engine. They looked at the bar as they drove past. The old lady was staring at them through the window.

'Let's get the hell out of here!' Geena said with relief, 'What a bunch of weirdos!'

'Nice beer though, and it was very cheap.'

'Yeah, but you don't know what they put in it! Don't fall asleep at the wheel will you? And let's see how your stomach is in a few hours!'

***

'Well my stomach's still okay,' Shawn remarked, 'No sign of poisoning. But it's very empty and I'm dying for another beer.'

'Mm, me too. Oh look, isn't that lovely! Let's go over there!' Geena pointed to a village perched on the edge of a mountain. Dazzling white houses jutted out over a sheer drop to a river far below in the valley.

Shawn stopped the car and took some photos, then they drove up a narrow curving road to the village.

Again they parked in the square beside the church.

'Which bar do you fancy this time?' Shawn asked.

'The nearest one to the church,' Geena said, 'They might have more love for their fellow men there.'

The bar was full. Everyone seemed to be shouting over everyone else and their voices ricocheted off the tiled floor and white walls. Two men were playing dominoes in the corner.

Silence fell when they spotted Shawn and Geena. A few of them nodded politely, then one by one they finished their drinks and left. Only the two men playing dominoes remained, hunched over their game.

Shawn ordered two beers and asked if they could have some food. The barman shook his head without speaking.

'Oh well, we'll have to go to another bar,' Shawn said, carrying their beers over to a table by the window, 'That's a shame isn't it?'

'Shawn,' Geena whispered, 'Have you noticed anything?'

'No, what?'

'That barman's the spitting double of the last one.'

'Probably his brother; or his cousin, six times over!'

'And I suppose that's his wife's sister!'

A woman in black with frown lines on her forehead had appeared beside the barman. Folding her arms, she studied Shawn and Geena.

'The people all look alike in these remote areas.' Shawn took a large swig of his beer. 'They dress alike, they eat the same meals at the same time, they intermarry and they never move far away from their families.'

Geena squealed and grabbed Shawn's hand. A little girl in a white dress skipped towards them, singing to herself. Spotting Shawn and Geena, she stopped and stared at them.

She looked so beautiful that Geena couldn't resist reaching her hand out.

The sweet innocent face was transformed. With a canine snarl the girl snapped at Geena's hand, then turned and ran as the woman shouted at her.

An old lady appeared from behind the bar and shuffled in their direction, a malevolent glare on her face. Geena stood up. 'I'm going,' she said.

'Aren't you going to finish your beer?' Shawn asked.

'No I'm not! There's something funny going on and I'm not waiting to find out what it is!'

Shawn followed her out and turned to shut the door. The old lady had just reached the door and she stared at them through the glass panel.

'What spooked you?' he asked as they drove away.

She stared at him, surprised. 'Didn't you notice? I could have sworn it was the same family that was in the last bar!'

Shawn burst out laughing. 'Don't be ridiculous! What do you think they did – followed us, then they waited to see which bar we chose, and rushed in the back and took over? I told you, they all look alike around here. And I'm starving!'

They drove slowly down the winding road.

'Okay, we're approaching another village,' Shawn said, 'Check behind us that we're not being followed, because I'm not going to leave another half-finished beer.'

'Ha ha, very funny.' But Geena didn't laugh. And she glanced behind them while Shawn parked the car in the village square.

They chose a bar and went inside. It was packed and noisy. Silence fell as they were noticed.

Several of the customers nodded and said, 'Hola.' Two men played dominoes in the corner. One of them looked up and nodded at them, then he continued with the game. Gradually everyone finished their drinks and left.

The barman came out of the kitchen and glared at them.

Geena gasped, grabbing hold of Shawn's arm. 'It's him, Shawn! The same barman!'

'Don't be daft,' Shawn muttered. But his voice was doubtful. And he was sure that he'd noticed a split second of recognition on the man's face.

He ordered two beers and asked if there was any food. The barman shook his head, so Shawn bought two packets of crisps.

Geena chose a table next to the door and reluctantly sat down on the edge of the seat. She kept glancing at the barman.

The barman called in to the kitchen. A woman dressed in black with frown lines on her face appeared and stood next to her husband. Folding her arms, she stared at Geena and Shawn.

A little girl in a white dress skipped out from behind the bar.

Geena jumped up, knocking her chair over. 'I'm getting out of here!' she cried, wrenching the door open with trembling hands.

'Hang on Geena!' Shawn called, rushing after her. He looked behind him apologetically, then froze, staring unbelieving at the old lady shuffling towards him, followed by the barman and his wife.

'Shawn, hurry!' Geena screamed and he leaped out, slamming the door behind him.

'Please hurry up!' Geena sobbed as Shawn tried to unlock the car.

Driving past the bar, they saw the family and the two dominoes players lined up at the window, watching them. They didn't move their heads; only their eyes followed the car travelling along the village street.

'Now do you believe me?' Geena asked, beggingly.

'I don't know what I believe,' Shawn replied. He wasn't joking any more.

***

'Where to now?' Shawn asked, pulling over and spreading out the map on the bonnet of the car.

'I'm starving, I'm thirsty, I'm tired and I've gone right off mountain villages,' Geena complained.

'Me too.' Shawn poked a finger at the map. 'There's a town here, about 10 kms away. We should be safe from interbred monsters there. And we need to find a room for the night.'

'Yes, and some food.'

'And a beer or two that I'm allowed to finish!'

***

They drove slowly along the deserted high street, looking for a place to stay. Geena pointed to a large, elegant building with a neon sign. 'A hotel! Safety! Food!'

Shawn reluctantly stopped the car. 'I thought we were going to stay in cheaper places.'

'I know, but…' Geena's eyes pleaded with him and Shawn turned the car into the curved drive and parked outside the hotel.

'Okay, but I'm checking out the staff very carefully before we book in. And if we're not greeted with a welcoming smile by someone who looks completely different to The Munsters of the mountains, we're not staying, agreed?'

'Agreed.' Geena smiled and linked arms with him.

The foyer was deserted. Large leather sofas and armchairs were grouped around the room and thick rugs were scattered over the floor. Everywhere was quiet.

'Oh this is much better,' Geena sighed, feeling the tension leave her. She was about to sink into an armchair when Shawn caught hold of her and kept her on her feet. 'Ah no, not yet. We haven't checked out the staff.'

A man emerged from a door behind the reception desk. He smiled warmly at them.

Geena sank into the armchair. 'They're checked,' she said, sighing with contentment and relief.

Shawn ordered a double room, two beers, and some food. The man nodded at every request and pointed for Shawn to sit down.

Sitting opposite Geena, Shawn stretched out his legs. He realised how scared he'd really been, although he hadn't wanted Geena to know. He looked at the man behind the desk and smiled gratefully.

The man smiled back, then he turned and called out through the door behind him.

Geena jumped up, shrieking, 'Shawn, that's one of the dominoes players!'

'Don't be-' Shawn began. Then the words froze on his lips as the barman appeared with a big smile on his face. He walked towards them, followed by his wife, the old lady, the little girl and the other dominoes player. They were all smiling.

The first dominoes player walked over to the front door. He locked and bolted it and closed the blind.

Shawn tried to stand but his legs wouldn't hold him up.

Collapsing back into the armchair, Geena pulled her knees up to her chin in a foetal position and closed her eyes, wrapping her arms over her head.

The smiling family gathered around them. The dominoes players pinched and poked Shawn, feeling his hair and face. Shawn started sobbing dry terrified sobs. His whole body was shaking.

Geena screamed again and again as the little girl scampered up on her lap like a puppy and sank her teeth deep into her neck.

Virtie

‘‘Ere you are son, I’ve brought yer a present,’ said his mum’s new boyfriend Wayne.

‘Aoooow, Jamie!’ shrieked Jamie’s mum. (She pronounced Jamie’s name ‘Jymie.’) ‘In’t that nice? Say thank you to yer Uncle Wayne.’ (She pronounced Wayne’s name ‘Whine.’)

The good things about Jamie’s mum’s latest boyfriends were that they nearly always brought Jamie presents at first, and his mum would be bubbling with happiness. The bad things were that they all wanted to ruffle his hair and have mock boxing-matches with him. And after a while they would start hitting his mum, or just vanish one day. Then she moped and complained until the next one came along, and it would all start again.

‘Thank you, Uncle Wayne,’ Jamie obediently chanted. He stared at the strange object in his hand. ‘Um, what is it?’ he asked.

‘It’s one of them virtual pets. I found it in a house clearance.’ Wayne spoke to Jamie’s mum. ‘The couple did a runner without paying their rent. They left all their stuff behind. The landlord kept it in his garage but he never heard a thing from them, so he got me to take the lot away.’

‘Some people are disgusting!’ yelled Jamie’s mum, looking unseeing at her filthy room. Jamie’s mum didn’t believe in housework. Her face lit up as a thought surfaced in her brain. A rare occurrence. ‘Ooow, I remember them things! Wasn’t they called tamagotchis or something?’ She smirked proudly at her knowledge.

‘What? Time I gotcha? Right, here I come then!’ Wayne waggled his fingers in the air and lumbered towards Jamie’s mum. She shrieked with delight and trotted slowly round the settee so that Wayne could catch her. He couldn't run very fast because of his beer-gut.

They collapsed on the settee and started noisily sucking each other's lips; a strange activity that Jamie's mum seemed to enjoy.

Jamie pressed the knob and stared, fascinated, as the tiny creature was 'born.' It rapidly developed and took shape and then it stared directly at Jamie and smiled.

'I'm going to look after you for ever and ever,' Jamie whispered. He glanced up to make sure that he wasn't being watched. He wasn't. His mum and Wayne were engrossed in each other. Raising the toy to his lips, he gently kissed the creature. He stared at it again. It stared back and winked at him.

'Mum! It winked at me!' he called.

'Yes! Oh yes!' gasped his mum.

'I'm going to call him Virtie and I won't let him die.'

'Yeah! Yeah! Oh Whine!' yelled his mum.

***

'I'm going to show all my friends what I've got,' Jamie announced the next morning.

'Yeah and I bet they'll all be dead jealous,' said Wayne, ruffling Jamie's hair before he could move out of reach. Then he burped and hitched his boxer shorts over his stomach.

Jamie's mum lit a cigarette and coyly blew smoke towards the ceiling. 'And you behave yourself,' she threatened with disinterest.

Wayne smiled at Jamie and winked. 'Leave 'im alone, he's a good kid!' He bunched his fists and, crouching in what he thought was a boxing position, he aimed mock punches at Jamie's chest. Jamie stepped back out of reach.

'Ooow Whine, you are funny! In't 'e funny, Jymie?'

Jamie agreed that, yes, Wayne was funny, as he backed out of the room.

Slamming the front door, Jamie dashed along the path, looking to see if he could spot any of his friends. One of his trainers (bought second-hand from a charity shop) came undone. He tripped over the lace, staggered a few steps, and landed face-down.

Fighting back his tears, he held Virtie up to check that it wasn't broken. No, thank goodness it was alright. Suddenly blood gushed out of his nose, running down his chin and onto his virtual pet.

Jamie overcame his fright and held his head back, pinching his nose until the blood stopped flowing, as his teacher did when anyone at school got a nosebleed.

A strange noise made him look down. He couldn't believe what he saw. Virtie was making a faint lapping sound and the toy wasn't covered in blood any more!

'Virtie!' Jamie gulped. The creature stared at Jamie and licked its lips.

***

What had woken him up? Jamie checked his dinosaur clock which had been a present from one of his mum's boyfriends a couple of years ago. The hands glowed in the dark. 2 o'clock.

Then he heard it; a faint whimpering sound. He reached onto his bedside cupboard that his mum had bought for 50p at a jumble sale, picked up his new toy and pressed the knob to feed it. The creature became quiet. Until 3am. Jamie fed it again, he held it as though to warm it, and he hung it round his neck and fell asleep.

He awoke at dawn. Something was wrong. Then he heard the faint lapping sound that had invaded his dreams. With a gasp Jamie sat up in bed. The toy had turned around in the night and it was stuck to Jamie's chest.

Jamie pulled it away and a trail of blood trickled down his stomach. He took the toy off and checked himself. It looked as though a spot on his chest had been scratched. He must have picked it in his sleep.

But what about the strange noise that had woken him? Jamie stared at Virtie who was licking its lips and staring directly at Jamie.

'Look, you mustn't do that,' Jamie whispered, 'It's wrong!'

The corners of the creature's mouth turned down and it made a faint whimpering noise. Jamie picked it up and pressed the knob to stop it crying, then he gently caressed it in his hand.

***

'I'm sure that thing's got bigger, hasn't it, Whine?'

Jamie hastily pushed the tamagotchi inside his teeshirt. 'Course it hasn't. They don't grow!'

'Not like little boys, eh? Eh?' Wayne ruffled Jamie's hair and bunched his fists, pretending to punch Jamie on the chest.

'Will you stop that?' Jamie muttered, peering down the front of his teeshirt.'

'You what?' asked Whine – I mean Wayne. (Sorry.)

'He's talking to his pet, ain't you Jymie? He thinks it's real!'

'No I don't!' Jamie protested.

'Well nothing them Japanese do would surprise me!' said Jamie's mum, collapsing onto Wayne's knee and lighting a cigarette.

'Ooh, shove up a bit to the left!' Wayne groaned.

'Um, I think I'll go and tidy my room.'

'You'll do what?!' squealed Jamie's mum, who never tidied anything except her hair.

'My room. It needs sorting out.' Jamie dashed into the hall and up the stairs, kicking aside the dirty washing and rubbish. He ripped the tamagotchi out of his teeshirt as he ran and rushed into his bedroom, flinging it onto his bedside cupboard. It started to cry.

'I've told you to stop biting me,' Jamie said, shaking a finger at the creature, 'And you can't still be hungry!'

'Jymie!' his mum screamed, 'Quick, come 'ere!'

He jumped and hastily pushed the toy under his pillow. Muffled whimpers followed him down the stairs.

His mum was in the kitchen, hopping up and down. 'Look what that bloody next-door's cat brought in!' she shrieked, clutching her knees.

'Where's Wayne?' asked Jamie, looking round the room. Surely he hadn't left her already?

'Gone down the pub to see a bloke about something. Get rid of it, Jamie!'

She ran into the garden and Jamie bent down to examine the tiny mouse. It was still wriggling. He picked it up by the tail and went to throw it outside. Then he hesitated.

He went upstairs to his bedroom and pulled Virtie out from under the pillow. 'Is this what you want?' he asked nervously.

The image of the creature became excited, jumping up and down. 'Feed me feed me feed me!' it demanded.

Jamie dropped the mouse on top of the toy and rushed out, trying not to listen to the sucking and crunching.

***

'Oy Jymie, come and see what yer Uncle Whine got down the pub!'

Curious, Jamie dashed down the stairs two at a time. And froze as the pitbull terrier bared its teeth and snarled at him.

'Now you stop that, Pongo!' Wayne shouted, ruffling its head and confusing the dog who didn't know if it was being praised or punished.

Thank goodness, Wayne might leave HIS head alone now, thought Jamie.

'Why do you call him Pongo, Whine?' Jamie's mum asked.

'Cos 'e stinks!' Wayne roared with laughter and Jamie's mum shrieked with delight, yelling, 'Aooow Whine!' and flinging her arms round Wayne's neck.

Disgusted, Jamie went back to his room and picked Virtie up. And tensed. What was that noise? Jamie threw Virtie under the bed.

A snuffling noise outside the door was followed by a bang as Pongo violently pushed the door open with his nose.

'Um, hello Pongo. Good dog,' said Jamie nervously, drawing his feet up out of the dog's reach.

Pongo paused, wondering why he was a good dog. Giving up, he growled menacingly. Then, curious, he snuffled under the bed.

There was a loud noise like bathwater going down the plughole. Pongo's hindquarters left the ground and the dog vanished under the bed without a squeak or a growl.

Jamie screwed his eyes shut and stuck his fingers in his ears until Virtie had finished eating and was quiet. Then he peeped under the bed. The virtual pet was fast asleep.

The only sign that Pongo had been there was a faint doggy whiff in the air.

***

'Jymie! Come down 'ere!'

Jamie went slowly down the stairs, trying to keep his face looking innocent.

''Ave you seen Pongo?' his mum asked him.

Jamie swallowed. 'No, Mum. I've been in my room.'

'I told you, you must 'ave left the front door open or something.'

'No Whine, I didn't. Honest!'

'Well that was a waste of a tenner then, wasn't it?' Wayne went back to reading the paper and Pongo was history.

***

The whimpering was louder and deeper. Jamie dragged himself awake and pressed the knob to feed Virtie.

The tamagotchi stayed in his bed all day (thank goodness his mum never made his bed!) and rested on his bedside cabinet at night. The toy was too big and heavy to hang round his neck now.

Three times in fifteen minutes Jamie had to feed it. Just pressing the knob didn't satisfy it for long any more.

At last it became quiet and Jamie sank into an exhausted sleep. His hand flopped out of the bed, hanging beside the bedside cupboard and the creature sucked happily at his finger, drinking his blood.

***

The toilet flushed but Jamie didn't hear it. He didn't hear his bedroom door open or see Wayne in his boxer shorts standing over him.

'Alright son?' asked Wayne, peering round the room. He couldn't figure out what he'd heard.

Sometime during the night Jamie had pulled his finger free in his sleep, knocking Virtie on the floor.

Hearing another strange sound, Wayne bent down, grunting with the effort.

'Bloody he-!' were his last words on this earth.

Jamie slept on; a deep, peaceful, anaemic sleep. He didn't hear the deep rumble from the floor, nor the munching and slurping, followed by a long-drawn-out contented burp.

Just as well really.

***

All of Jamie's savings from his Star Wars money box (a present from his mum's boyfriend before last) was spent at the supermarket. Virtie was fond of raw liver, and it had satisfied the creature for a few days. But its demands had grown again and Jamie was broke.

Jamie decided to let his pet die. He stuck it under his bed and tried to ignore its plaintive cries for food. He also tried to ignore his mum's plaintive cries. 'Aooow, Whine!' she'd whine. 'D'yer know, Jymie, I really thought 'e was the one,' she sighed, lighting a cigarette and collapsing onto a kitchen chair, 'At least 'e could have said goodbye, instead of sneaking away in the night!'

Jamie nodded solemnly and fixed his gaze on a rusty shopping trolley at the end of the garden. He wasn't sure what had happened to Wayne, but he had his suspicions as Virtie had slept so well after Wayne had disappeared.

'Don't worry Mum, I'll look after you,' he assured her.

'Ow Jymie, you're such a good boy,' said his mum, reaching out and ruffling his hair.

***

'Jymie!'

Gasping, Jamie woke up. 'What?'

'Give yer poor mum a cuddle, my special boy!' Jamie's mum sobbed. She flopped onto the bed, bouncing Jamie off the mattress. Her breath smelt of gin, as it always did after a broken romance.

'Let's go in your room, Mum,' Jamie suggested, trying to get out of bed.

Jamie's mum stood up, hiccoughed, staggered, and slid under the bed.

'Mum!' Jamie screamed, 'No Virtie! Naughty! Let my mum go!' He tried to grab his mum's shoulders but she disappeared too fast.

He turned round and looked down at the other side of the bed, hoping to see his mum sliding out. But she didn't.

Virtie dined happily, making contented munching noises. Then it began to snore, relaxed and satisfied.

For a while.

Jamie drew his knees up to his chin and stuck his thumb in his mouth.

It was time to do some Serious Thinking.

About the Author

Lyn Funnell has been passionate about writing for most of her life. At school, she almost always earned a gold or silver star for her weekly compositions.

Her first publications appeared in magazines, followed by twelve collections of short stories and poetry. Many of her short stories feature an unexpected twist, and her work has won several prizes.

Beyond writing, Lyn enjoys entering competitions and has received numerous accolades for her original recipes. Her achievements include winning The Good Housekeeping Millennium Menu competition and being a runner-up in the BBC Chef of the Year competition. She was also one of three runners-up in the Observer Food & Drink Magazine competition and has won prizes in the Fruits of France Recipe, Ocean Spray Cranberry Recipe, Bernard Matthews Rustle Up a Recipe, and Dorling Kindersley Autumn Recipe competitions.

Additionally, she reached the semi-finals of Masterspud and was one of three finalists in The BBC One Show Spag

Bol Competition, earning her the title of UK Spag Bol Queen!

To date, Lyn has published a total thirteen books. *Dark Delights* and the previous two books have been via Michael Terence Publishing.

Lyn lives in East Sussex and co-runs the online magazine Unknown Kent and Sussex:

www.unknownkentandsussex.co.uk

and The Write Site:

www.the-write-site.com

Available worldwide from Amazon
and all good bookstores

Michael Terence
Publishing
www.mtp.agency

www.facebook.com/mtp.agency

@mtp_agency

Printed in Dunstable, United Kingdom

65855537R00082